HAVEN 4
by Misty Vixen

PROLOGUE

David couldn't remember the last time he had been so thoroughly at a loss for words.

He stared at Cait, his mouth open slightly, her words ringing in his head. For once, he wasn't falling silent because he wasn't sure which words to choose, sorting through one phrase after another. No, this time, nothing came. His mind felt blank.

All around him, no one spoke, all eyes on the two of them.

Finally, after what felt like a very long time, he said, "Are you sure?"

Cait laughed, and so did several of the other women. "Yes, David. I'm sure."

"That you're pregnant?" he asked, still grappling with the knowledge that had just been presented to him.

She laughed again and gave his hands a gentle squeeze. "Yes, David. That's what my trip to the doctors was about. And just to save you the trouble of asking, yes I'm sure it's yours. You're the only human man I've been with in a good six months."

"When...did it happen?" he murmured.

"Ironically," she said, smirking, "the very first night we met. Remember? I *begged* you to get me pregnant, and apparently you obliged."

"Holy shit," he whispered. "I'm...you're going to be a mother?" She nodded. "And I'm...going to be a father?" She nodded again. "...holy shit. I need...wow. This is...very unexpected."

That got more laughter.

David seemed to remember suddenly that he was in a roomful of people and he looked around at all of them. Evelyn and April and Lara were standing together. April looked a little nervous, but generally happy. Evelyn and Lara were practically beaming. As was Ashley. Jennifer had a small smile on her face. And Ellie…

He frowned. Ellie looked like she was going to be sick.

Ellie was staring at him and Cait like someone had just told her they had died.

Before he could say anything else, she suddenly set down the cup she was holding and began striding rapidly across the room, towards the stairwell.

"Ellie? Where are you going?" Cait asked, letting go of his hands. She apparently didn't hear her because she just kept walking. "Ellie?" Cait asked, more loudly.

Ellie froze at the bottom of the stairs. She turned to face them and said, "Congratulations." Then she all but sprinted up the stairs.

"What the fuck?" David whispered.

"I don't know," Cait said, and took off after her.

He followed in her wake. The two of them hurried up the stairs. Getting up top, they looked down the length of the hallway and saw the door to Cait's and Ellie's shared bedroom open. She was moving around inside, barely visible in the moonlight coming in through the window. They hurried down the hallway.

"Ellie, what are you doing?" Cait asked as they came to stand in the doorway.

She was shoving things into her pack.

"I-I need to go," she said. She looked on the verge of panic.

"Ellie, what's *wrong?*" Cait demanded, stepping forward. She reached out to touch her, then stopped short, hesitated, and pulled her hand back.

"I just need to go," Ellie repeated. She zipped up her pack and threw it on.

"Ellie, wait! Talk to me, please! What's wrong?" Cait asked.

Ellie finally turned to look at them. "I'm sorry. I know this is unexpected, but I have to leave. I just-I need to be by myself for a while. I'm sorry." She walked stiffly to the window, opened it, and then looked back at them. "Don't try to look for me, and don't expect me back."

"For how long?!" David asked.

"I don't know." She paused one more time, looking back at them with a look of remorse, regret, and anguish.

"I'm sorry," she repeated, and then she slipped nimbly out the window.

They both hurried over to it and looked out, watching her hit the ground and slip off to the perimeter fence, where she slid easily through a gap in it.

And then she was disappearing into the frozen forest, and she was gone.

"What the fuck just happened?" David whispered.

"I have an idea," Cait replied. She sighed softly, her breath foaming on the chilled air that streamed in through the window. He looked over at her. She looked ghostly and painfully beautiful in the pale moonlight, but also very sad. She shivered and then closed and locked the window.

"Ellie..." She paused, then sat down on her bed. David sat down beside her, waiting. "A lot happened to her. She told me things that I won't repeat, but bad things happened to her. And it broke her. And I think...I'm not sure, really, but I think my announcement scared the shit out of her. Maybe she thought she was losing me, and she couldn't handle that."

She heaved a sigh suddenly and looked at him. "We'll deal with that soon, but right now...tell me. Tell me what you're thinking about..." She looked down and laid a hand carefully over her stomach. "...about this."

"I-I don't know," he admitted. "I'm worried. If I'm being honest. I-I didn't expect this! I didn't even think it was possible!"

"I know," she said, a small smile on her face. "I wasn't sure whether or not I could even get pregnant, and I remember you saying you were pretty sure you couldn't get a girl pregnant. Obviously that isn't true." She hesitated. "Do you believe me? That it's yours?"

"Oh yes," he replied immediately. "I believe you. I don't think you would lie to me about that. I'm just...this is a lot. Especially after all that happened tonight."

"I know. I'm sorry to just throw it out there like that, but I couldn't hold it in any longer. I needed you to know. But there's more I need you to know, David." She gently placed a finger under his chin and raised his face so that they locked eyes.

"If you don't want to be a part of this child's life, then I won't hold that against you. You were not ready for this, you didn't ask for this. I understand that. I've already come to terms with this: I want to be a mother. I think I've always wanted that, but I just never truly thought about it until I got the news. But this wasn't...expected. I'm not going to try and force this responsibility on you, because this is going to alter the course of my life, and yours, if you decide you want to be a part of this child's life."

David thought about it, staring at her. There were so many things to consider, so many difficulties with raising a child even under the best of circumstances, let alone the post-apocalyptic nightmare they now found themselves in.

And yet, could he ask for a better mother for his child? Cait was...so many things. Smart, kind, compassionate, brave, fun, dedicated, loving. But he didn't doubt for a second that she wanted to raise a child, looking at her in the moonlight. There was no turmoil there, no uncertainty. Just a peace, a tranquility in her eyes, an acceptance, a happy acceptance.

In that moment, David suddenly had his answer. He didn't know why he had arrived at the conclusion he had, especially knowing there was so much to consider, but wasn't that how it went sometimes?

Hell, maybe even most of the time?

People usually went with their gut. A lot of people said they wanted to reason things out, make informed decisions, and while he still believed in that, he believed, especially right now, that sometimes the decision got made for you. Like love. He hadn't *decided* that he was going to start falling in love with Cait, or Evelyn, or April, and yet he was. He could tell he was.

In the same way, he knew that how he felt about becoming a father wasn't a decision, not really, not in this case, at least. Regardless of his own actions, Cait was pregnant with his child. And he knew in some immutable way that he wanted to be her partner, wanted to raise the child with her, wanted to be a father.

All that came out of his mouth was: "Yes."

As if she could read his mind, she immediately hugged him tightly against her. "Thank you," she whispered. She held him to her. "You're going to be a wonderful father, David. I haven't met anyone else in my life that I wish had gotten me pregnant."

"Oh, well I'm glad," he replied.

She laughed loudly and pulled back. She sniffed and wiped at her eyes. He blinked a few times and realized, abruptly, that he had a few tears of his own.

"Emotional times," Cait muttered, wiping at her eyes.

"I guess so," he said, doing the same. Something abruptly occurred to him. "Oh shit!" he said, shooting to his feet.

"What? What's wrong?" Cait asked.

"I fucked Ashley and Lara! What if they're–"

"Oh! David, no. Don't worry," she said, reaching out. She took his hand and he let her pull him gently back down onto the bed. "I already talked with them about it. That's why I asked you about your sexual partners. Do you honestly think I'd have let you fuck Lara tonight if she wasn't fixed? No, don't worry. They have both confirmed that, without a doubt, they can't get pregnant. So don't worry, I'm the only one you've knocked up."

"Oh...okay then. Good."

He kissed her, then he looked back through the door. "Shit, we shouldn't keep the others in suspense."

"Oh right. Fuck." She sighed heavily and looked out the window again. "Goddamnit, Ellie," she whispered.

"What are we going to do?" he asked.

"Let her be," Cait replied. "I might be able to

find her, if I tried hard, but I doubt it. And she doesn't want to be found. She needs time. And..." she looked regretful, "...and we might need to be prepared to never see her again."

"What? Seriously?!"

"Yes. I don't know if it's likely, but I think...I just don't know if she can handle this. Obviously she can't right now, given that she just jumped out a window. But regardless, we have to let her be. We have to let her work this out on her own."

He looked out the window, a cold, heavy weight of loss and remorse settling on his heart, as if this was somehow his fault.

Hell, in a way, he supposed it kind of was.

"I'll miss her," he said softly.

"I know. I will, too. We just have to hope that she gets it sorted out, and that she comes back to us." Cait stood suddenly. "Come on."

He stood with her and they made their way downstairs, where they found the others talking quietly among themselves.

"What happened?" Evelyn asked.

Cait sighed heavily. "Ellie...needs to be alone for a little while. I'm not sure when she'll be back. Officially speaking: we should not be relying on her help until she returns."

"Oh my God," April whispered. "Is she...okay?"

"I don't know," Cait admitted.

"I know it's *really* nosy and probably rude to ask but...I mean, how *do* you feel about this?" Lara asked suddenly, looking at David.

He stepped closer to Cait, slipped one arm around her torso, and laid his other hand against her belly. "We're having a child," he said.

That got a great reaction out of everyone. For a

few moments, as everyone came closer and began to congratulate them and hug and kiss both of them, the weight of the events that had transpired tonight, from the incredibly risky assault to the near death experiences to Ellie up and leaving, seemed to fall away.

He lost himself in the moment and as he looked around at the others, standing together in this warm building in the middle of the night, knowing that there were others in cabins very close by, it gave him a feeling of tremendous, overwhelming joy and comfort, something that he wasn't sure he had ever actually felt before.

This felt like…

A home.

It felt like a haven that he could rest in, hide from the world in, build a life in.

As he looked at Evelyn and April, though, a new feeling came to him, and he knew that they were going to have to talk about this sudden development, because it would likely have serious impacts on their lives, too.

"We should probably, uh, talk," he said, looking at them both.

Evelyn just smiled. "Tomorrow," she said. "You two need sleep. You look like death warmed over. We *all* need sleep, actually, because we've got a shitload of work ahead of us tomorrow and the day after that. You two, I imagine, will want to get some intimate time together. So...sleeping arrangements. April, will you be willing to sleep with me and give up your bed for the night?"

"Yes," she said.

"Okay. Lara, how about you take her bed?" Evelyn suggested.

"I appreciate it," Lara replied.

"Okay. Jennifer..." She frowned, no doubt considering it. They actually didn't have much in the way of accommodations.

"I saw a couch in the main room, I can sleep there," Jennifer said.

"Are you sure?" Evelyn asked.

"Yes. As a wraith, I don't even actually need to sleep per se, though I wouldn't mind in this case. But I can sleep on the floor, this will be fine," Jennifer replied.

"Okay. I'll get you a pillow and a blanket. Get some sleep everyone. We're going to want to get to that outpost as soon as we can tomorrow," Evelyn said.

David sighed. "Yeah, good point."

"I guess that means I gotta go home and sleep in my own bed?" Ashley asked.

"You can sleep in mine," Evelyn replied.

"*Yes,*" she whispered, making Evelyn laugh.

David went around and gave each woman a hug and a kiss, and told them all goodnight. Lara lingered on the kiss. "I had a lot of fun," she said. "A *lot* of fun."

"So did I. You are *great* in bed, and an *amazingly* sexy and beautiful woman," he replied.

She smiled and blushed. "Shut up."

"I'm not lying."

She looked like she was trying not to smile, but she just shook her head. "I believe that you believe it, at least."

"You're definitely hot," Cait said, coming up next to him.

She sighed. "Okay, whatever. Just show me to my bed." Her expression turned glum. "As much as

I'd love to stick around and help out, I really need to get back home after this."

"I understand, I'll miss you, though," David replied.

"I'll miss you, too. Don't worry, I'm sure I'll visit."

April led her off upstairs after that, showing her to her room, and Evelyn tracked down some bedding for Jennifer, setting her up on the couch. After making sure that the area was secure, the doors locked and the windows shut, David and Cait went upstairs to her bedroom. They pushed the door most of the way closed, then began undressing.

"So, Lara was a good fuck then?" Cait asked.

"A *great* fuck," he replied. "Her thighs...*damn*. So sexy. Not as sexy as yours though."

She laughed. "You don't need to reassure me. I'm not that kind of girl. Speaking of my thighs though...you know my ass is going to probably get really fat, and my hips and thighs are going to thicken up, and my tits are gonna get huge, right?"

"They already are," he muttered, but he couldn't help but think about what Cait would look like pregnant. Like, noticeably pregnant.

He'd seen pregnant women before, and they never failed to turn him on *so* hard.

"My belly's gonna grow a lot, too. I'm gonna get stretch marks," she said.

"I don't care. You're going to look *so* hot pregnant, and you'll still be wicked hot after."

She smiled. "You're a sweetheart." As she finished stripping, she stepped up to him and settled her hands on his back. "There's also a decent chance that I will be *super* horny. Like, more so than I am right now on average. So you're going to need to fuck me even more than you do now," she said with a sultry smile.

"I think I can manage that," he replied, and she laughed, then she kissed him.

It was in that moment that her lips met his that he realized something had changed. He wasn't sure if it was that he had done the most decisive thing of his life in helping plan for, enact, and execute that strike on the thieves, the fact that he had risked his life, or the fact that he knew he was to be a father.

Possibly, probably even, it was all three, but he thought it was that third one most of all. Something had changed between them, and for the better. From the way her eyes widened slightly and how she pressed herself more closely against him, David could tell that something had changed for Cait, too.

He held her, leaning her back slightly and deepening the kiss, and she moaned. They began to make out with an intense passion, running their hands across each other. Her skin felt so hot against his in the pale moonlight, as if it was a physical manifestation of her passion, her lust, her desire.

David pushed her onto her back and she landed with an easy grace in the bed, opening her legs smoothly for him, smiling up at him, her face illuminated by the moonlight. She looked achingly beautiful, impossibly gorgeous in that ghostly light, and he immediately climbed onto her, *needing* to be inside of her.

Normally their sessions were longer, and foreplay was very standard between them, but sometimes it was like this, where they simply *needed* to be making love. He needed to be inside of her as much as she needed him to be inside of her. And he could see her practically glistening, she was so wet.

Before he could even get into position, she reached down between them, gripped his cock, and slipped it inside of herself.

"*Ohhhh, David...*" she gasped, her voice thick with emotion and love and lust.

"Cait," he moaned as he penetrated her, "oh, Cait. Oh my fucking...oh *Cait!*"

He pushed deep into her, and she immediately wrapped her legs around his waist. He began to make desperate, impassioned love to her and she stared up at him with wide, unblinking blue eyes that seemed to glow from within. He had never quite seen this expression on her face before, or maybe it was just the intensity of it.

David was sure that he had a similar expression. He began to thrust wildly into her and she moaned loudly, pulling him down, and they resumed kissing. The pleasure ate him alive. He boiled in it, was melted by it, and loved every second of its consumption of him. Cait felt like a living goddess of sex and lust and beauty as he made increasingly frantic love to her, driving furiously into her now.

The sounds she made…

Neither of them lasted long. It was a short but ferocious session. Cait began to orgasm in under a minute, and she screamed into the kiss, unwilling or maybe even unable to break it, to release him, and he moaned loudly as he felt her insides clench hard around him, felt that hot release of sex juices. And he moaned, and lost himself completely, and began to orgasm barely five seconds after she had begun to.

He pumped her sweet, perfect pussy full of his seed, immediately releasing a hot spurt that surged into her, and then another, and another, draining himself into her, filling her up. She moaned louder, accepting it all, almost begging for it with her body.

They came together, and for some brief but seemingly timeless moment, became lost together, entangled within each other, bathed in pure ecstasy.

When they had finished, he laid on top of her and didn't pull out for a long time.

There was so much to say, but as the minutes drifted by in the moonlit comfort of her room, they remained locked inside of his head, and no doubt in hers as well. Not forever, but for now. He almost fell asleep before he spoke. Almost, but not quite.

"Cait?" he asked softly.

"Yes?" she murmured, slowly running one hand up and down his bare back.

"It's different now, isn't it?"

"Yes, David. It is."

"And not just because you're pregnant."

"No."

"We need to get more serious, don't we?"

"Yes, we do."

He almost didn't say the thing that wanted to escape his lips. Almost. But then, in the quiet of their shared space, he whispered, "Cait?"

"Yes, David?"

"...I love you."

They weren't looking at each other, not exactly. He had his head on the pillow, facing her, and she was laying on her back, staring out the window, so he could only see a portion of her beautiful, pale face.

But he saw her smile. "I know. I love you too, David."

And he hugged her tightly to him, and she hugged him back. He pulled out of her and laid on his side. They embraced once more, facing each other.

That was how they fell asleep.

CHAPTER ONE

When David opened his eyes the next morning, he prepared himself for the wave of groggy lethargy that was surely to come from perhaps five hours of sleep.

He'd had to push through the misery of not enough sleep many times in his life. But as he found himself looking up at the old, pitted wooden ceiling of Cait's room, the sunshine streaming in through the window, all he felt was exuberance. He felt *energized*.

He also had a steel hard-on and was feeling hornier than usual.

Cait was nude and hot and pressed up against him, and it didn't take long for his hands to start running over her soft, warm body beneath the blankets. Were her tits already bigger? When did that happen?

She had to be about a month along now, if she got pregnant that very first time they had sex...David realized he knew so little about pregnancy. He honestly didn't think it was a thing he'd ever have to be involved with.

He pushed Cait onto her back and got between her legs, and she let out a loud moan as he slid into her.

She was *so* wet.

"Oh, *David...*" she moaned as he pushed his way inside of her, burying his whole length into her. "Give it to me..." she begged.

He started to thrust deep and hard into her, and she let out a loud cry of ecstasy.

The session didn't last long.

David felt pumped up and full of energy, and he was maddened with lust, hugging her tightly to him as he pounded her brains out. But beneath that, though, he was impatient. He wanted to get to work. He wanted to get this lust out of him, clear his mind, and focus on the day ahead. Because there was so much work to be done.

But in that moment, he really just wanted to fucking come inside of her, because that was the best feeling in the entire world.

He got his wish hardly a minute and a half later when Cait began to orgasm intensely against him, and it set him off into a blindingly powerful climax of his own. He listened to her shout and yell and groan incoherently with bliss, his own voice adding to the clamor as he emptied himself into her, pumping out his seed into her amazing pussy.

And then they were done, coming down from the high of rapture, panting for breath.

"Oh my," she whispered after a bit, "that was...that's...oh wow."

"Yes," he murmured.

"It's different now," she said, echoing his sentiment from last night, as if confirming it. "It's different now."

"Do you like that?"

"I love it." She smiled ruefully at him. "Remember this, please, when I'm puking and pissed at you, accusing you of doing this to me. Remember that I'm happy this happened. I wasn't seeking it or planning on it, but...I am happy that I got pregnant, and that it's you that did it."

"I'm happy, too," he murmured. "And I'll keep it in mind." He pulled out of her and got up. "And now, we've got a lot of work to do."

"Yes. I *would* like to get as much done as possible while I can still run and jump, let alone walk," Cait said.

"I have a hard time imagining anything stopping you from going out there," David replied as he tracked down their washbasin and set to cleaning up.

Cait sighed softly. "I *am* going to have to make sacrifices. I can't do crazy shit all the time now. I mean, I *will* if we're being threatened, but I can't take irresponsible risks anymore. I've got a kid on the way and you and Evelyn and April and...Ellie."

They were silent for a moment, then she got up and began cleaning up with him.

"Do you think she's really leaving? Like, not coming back?" David asked quietly.

Cait sighed again. "I don't know," she admitted. "I thought she might be uncomfortable with my pregnancy, but I didn't think she'd flip her shit like that. Right now, I think *she* doesn't know if she's leaving or not. But what I really think is that we should take her advice at face value: don't expect her to show up."

"I just don't get it," he muttered.

"I know. Let's just say that it's complicated, and that I don't get it fully, either. Unfortunately, we're going to have to rely on ourselves for now, and just...hope."

"I *do* hope she comes back. I...like her," he murmured.

"I like her, too. A lot."

They fell silent as they finished washing and drying off. As they started dressing, she noticed him looking at her belly.

She laughed softly. "David, you can't see anything yet."

"I know," he replied, then, before she could get her shirt on, he stepped up to her and gently laid a hand against her stomach. "I'm just...still surprised by all this."

"I can tell. I am, too." She placed her hand over the back of his, then she kissed him and began to pull her shirt on. "Come on, we can't keep getting distracted."

"Yeah," he agreed as his drive and focus found him again.

There was *so* much to do.

At least he was lucky enough to know where to begin.

David and Cait pulled their clothes on and headed into the hallway. "I'm going to go do a round and make sure everything's okay," Cait said.

"Okay, I'm going to get started on breakfast," David replied.

Cait headed downstairs and David slipped into the kitchen area. No one seemed to be up yet. That was rare, usually *someone* was up before him. Well, usually it was Ellie, he supposed. That was going to change.

Not just because she was gone, (forever? Really?), but because he was going to have to start getting serious about how he managed his life. Because he wasn't just responsible for himself, or even just for a few others, but for now a whole group of people. Maybe responsible wasn't exactly the right word.

It wasn't like they lived or died by his actions, or that he was their superior, but his actions would certainly either help or hinder them. And, he had to admit, more so now because there was no getting around it: they looked to him as a leader.

He intended to help them as much as possible.

David slipped into the kitchen and got to work. He got a fire going first in the wood-burning stove, then began pulling out food. Bacon and eggs, mostly. It was a simple but hearty breakfast. He also pulled out a bit of sausage. As he began the process of frying it up, he heard a small sound, almost like a squeak, and he turned.

"Frostbite," he murmured.

Their little pet mouse, inasmuch as he *was* a pet, sat on his haunches a few feet behind David. He twitched his whiskers and stared up at him with his little eyes.

"Are you hungry?" he asked.

Frostbite squeaked after a moment, more insistently.

David laughed. "I'll take that as a yes." He pulled off some sausage and then slowly turned around and crouched down. Carefully, he extended his hand, palm flat and facing up, onto the floor. "I'll make you a deal. You can have this sausage if you let me hold you."

He knew it was a little bit of a risk. Frostbite might stick true to his name and bite him, but he didn't think the little white mouse would.

The mouse hesitated, sniffing the air, then began to come closer. His movements were cautious at first, but eventually he came up to David's hand. He thought the mouse would snatch the food out of his hand and scurry off, but Frostbite actually climbed into his palm. He began to nibble on the sausage.

"Okay, now I'm going to pet you," he said, and carefully brought his other hand closer.

Frostbite hesitated, then resumed eating. David laid one finger gently against Frostbite's head, then began to run it down his back.

His fur was soft. Frostbite stiffened briefly, then once again resumed eating.

"There you go," he whispered. "This deal worked out quite nicely," he murmured, and stroked the mouse's fur a few more times.

He heard movement at the same time he caught some out of the corner of his eye. So did Frostbite apparently, because he finished his meal and then hopped off David's hand, scurrying towards a hole in the wall.

Lara stood at the entrance to the kitchen, her eyes wide. "Oh my fucking God, David. That was the cutest thing I've ever fucking seen in my life," she said.

He chuckled and stood back up, then went about washing his hands. "You were there the whole time?" he asked.

"Yes. Don't be embarrassed. That was wonderful," she replied.

"I'm a little...I didn't think anyone was there," he said.

She crossed the room. "Come on, don't be embarrassed," she repeated, standing before him. "Believe it or not, I actually prefer a man who pets cute little mice when he thinks no one's looking. The only thing that's better is when he pets cute little mice regardless of who's looking. Why are you embarrassed?"

"It's..." He sighed. "Weakness isn't well tolerated, in case you somehow missed out on that. Either that or its taken advantage of."

"I'm not going to take advantage of you," she said. He looked at her. She looked remarkably sexy in her military uniform, her brown hair smoothed down, her blue eyes sparkling in the morning sunlight.

"It's not that. It's just...it's a little different, with you."

"Why?"

"I guess it shouldn't be, given the company I keep. I don't know. You're in the military, or, you know, what's left of it. Soldiers have a reputation." He shook his head suddenly. "Don't mind me, I'm being stupid. I don't mind that you saw. It just caught me off guard." Maybe that was a lie, but he didn't feel like arguing with her.

"It's okay, I get it." She gave him a hug and looked like she was going to kiss him, then hesitated. "I guess I should ask. Kiss?"

"Please, yes," he replied immediately.

She laughed and kissed him, and he kissed back, feeling that wonderful sensation of locking lips with a beautiful woman. "That was nice," she murmured when they stopped. "I guess I shouldn't be worried about anything?"

"Between us? Hell no. Last night was amazing, you're amazing, I just hope you enjoyed yourself as much as you appeared to," he replied, moving back over to the food and tending to it.

"Oh, I did. That you can be sure of. I guess I was just a little paranoid. Although I guess I shouldn't be. Cait was remarkably open with me. I'd say that the pregnancy might change things, but she told me she was pregnant around the same time she told me I should go ride your cock."

He laughed. "Did she really say that?"

"Basically. She thought you would be amazingly into me. And she seemed to be right."

"Oh yeah, she was right. You are...fantastically attractive. In a number of ways."

She laughed softly and looked away. "I'm glad you think so."

"You want some breakfast?"

"As much as I appreciate a man making me breakfast after banging my brains out, I'm afraid I have to go. I'm certainly in enough trouble as it is, since I have no doubt Stern saw through whatever excuse I made yesterday to come help you," she replied.

"Here, take some bacon at least, this one's about done," he said, setting it on a plate to cool for a moment.

"Thanks," she murmured.

"Listen, Lara...if things ever go bad there, or if you just decide you're sick of their shit, you can come here. I mean, obviously we could use someone like you. You're smart, you're fast, you're brave. You're obviously a great shot. But you're a good person and if you really wanted it to be, this could be a home for you."

She looked startled, silent for several seconds. Finally, she cleared her throat. "I appreciate that," she said, regaining her composure. "I...none of you are what I expected. But, um, I'll take that to heart." She grabbed the bacon, began to leave, then hesitated. "Is Ellie really gone? Did she just...leave?" she asked.

David sighed. "It's looking that way. She literally jumped out the window after grabbing all her shit. I'm not really sure what's going on with her, but..." He shrugged.

"That really sucks...well, thanks for the bacon. And the sex. It was great. I'm not sure when I'll be able to see you again, but you can rest assured that I do intend to see, and fuck, you again."

"I'm very much looking forward to it," he

replied.

She just smiled and started heading out, eating the bacon he'd made.

David turned back to the meal. By the time he was finished, everyone else had come into the dining area. Evelyn, Cait, April, Ashley, and Jennifer all gathered around the table, talking animatedly about what had happened last night, and about Cait's pregnancy.

While he still felt good about his decision to be a partner to her and help her raise their child, he knew that he needed time for it to really sink in, because he still felt just...out of it, with regards to the news. It was just so unexpected, it had blindsided him thoroughly.

He finished making the food and brought it out to the table, where the others thanked him and dug in hungrily.

"Okay," he said after he'd eaten some of his own meal. "So, today is going to be about getting all the shit from the thieves' camp to here. We need to grab as much of it as we can. April, I'm going to leave you in charge of the campgrounds, while everyone else is coming with me. Unless someone has a better idea?"

"You sure you want to leave me in charge?" April asked uncertainly.

"Yes," David replied. "You can handle it, April. I remember you told Evelyn and I to...help you out, with regards to that. I'm confident you can do this. And, worst case scenario, you can ask Amanda for help. She seems pretty competent and willing to help out."

"Yeah," Cait said, "she'll definitely help you. Don't worry, April." She reached across the table and took her hand. "You can do this."

She looked over at Cait, then around the table at them, then slowly nodded. "Yeah, okay. I'll handle it."

"Thank you, April," David replied. "And we'll be coming back throughout the day, I'm sure. Plus, you'll have a whole group of people here, too."

"I'll make it work," April said, and she sounded a bit more confident this time.

"Excellent. Now, let's finish up and grab our gear. The longer we wait, the longer that stuff sits there to be taken."

They all began eating a little faster.

...

As he walked among the frozen trees, beneath the sunlight, surrounded by snow and ice, David couldn't help but come back to what he had said to Cait last night.

It's different now.

That was true in more ways than he initially realized. The victory against the assholes who had burned down River View seemed to have changed something in him. He thought that it was probably the most decisive thing he had ever done in his entire life. He'd helped enact a plan, a big, risky plan, and it had actually worked.

That felt…

Powerful.

But not just in a 'I'm strong' kind of way. No. More in a 'I can actually *do* shit' kind of way. He felt like he could actually enact plans, he could actually make things *happen*. Before last night, the idea of converting those campgrounds into a new settlement, even a small one, seemed fundamentally daunting and even impossible.

It seemed like one of those faraway, 'someday' goals. Not something that you actively worked towards day-to-day and achieved in the near future. But he was beginning to think that he could at least *do* this.

He could, if he set his mind to it, and persisted, and had the right people helping him out who were also persistent, make the campgrounds into a real home. A place people could live and grow and be safe from the miserable hellish wasteland the world had become. David looked around as he heard a distant gunshot, and a few far-off warning growls in response to the sudden noise. It would be difficult, though.

It would be the hardest thing he had ever done, and it would take...a very long time.

Because it wasn't just something you did and then it was over. No, it was something you maintained. Something you *kept* doing. Something you committed to doing every single day. Like raising a child.

It would be hard, very hard, but it felt worth doing. He wanted to do it. And that's probably where this energy, this vitality he felt buzzing through him, was coming from. Not just the knowledge that it was going to be very difficult, not just that he wanted to do it, but the knowledge that he was going to have to really step up his game. He was going to have to buckle down, focus, and work his fucking ass off to make this happen.

David looked around at the others. At Evie, at Cait and Jennifer, at Ashley. He thought about April, back home. Ellie, out there somewhere. Lara, heading back to her base. Amanda and the people who were now living in the campgrounds. At the very least, he owed it to them to give this his all. To put in that effort.

He had lived on his own before, he'd done the whole 'think about only yourself' thing more than once, for long stretches of time. And honestly, he was just tired of it. He didn't want to be alone anymore.

He didn't want to be alone ever again, not in the way he had been before.

He wanted a home he could come back to. A fixed point in the world that was *his*. That he shared with other people that he loved.

Loved.

He had told Cait that he loved her, and she had said it back to him. Although he knew it to be true, and he believed her...

David glanced again at Evelyn.

This was something they were going to have to discuss, because she had come first, as had April, and because this...was not in their plan. Although they had all agreed to date each other, he recognized that there was indeed a difference between dating someone and impregnating them. It felt like there was a power shift now, and he didn't know how to handle that, or even if he *could*. Now that he knew he loved Cait, he knew what that meant and what that felt like, he knew that he felt the same way towards Evie and April.

Which meant he loved them, too.

But was it different? Although he had no intention of loving any of them more than the other, Evie or April might not feel that way, given he wasn't even capable of having a child with them. This was *definitely* something he was going to have to discuss with them.

He began pondering over how to handle *those* particular conversations, and still didn't have something he felt comfortable with by the time they were coming up on the hunting grounds encampment.

He felt his heart skip a beat as he spied a few figures moving between the buildings, but relaxed as he realized they were zombies. They could deal with zombies. The group split up and moved in, then got to it. Hardly a minute went by before they had made quick work of the undead, shooting all they saw in the head, and then putting down the handful more that came out of any hiding places they'd gotten into.

David looked around. In the cold light of day, the place looked pretty bad. A lot of stray rounds had punched into the buildings, and there was a lot of blood on the walls, and a lot of bodies laying around. Most of the windows had been broken out, too. Everything had a cold, dead feeling to it. Though David could see a few telltales that someone with intention had been through. Hopefully they hadn't taken too much.

"Well," he said with a sigh, "let's get to it."

They all set to work, each picking one of the buildings that helped make up an impromptu perimeter to the hunting grounds camp and beginning their search. There was so much they would have to investigate, between the buildings here, the bodies scattered across the camp and the outlying areas, and the few other buildings that happened to be nearby. It was going to be a very long haul, and all of it done in the cold.

But it was worth doing, because even at a glance, David could see a lot of supplies. Between this and the haul they'd gotten last night, this was the kind of thing that would offer them security as a group for weeks or even months, if they were smart enough about rationing it out, and be lucky enough to get some good trades.

Mainly, though, were the guns. There were a lot of guns. That was going to help them so much, because you could find and grow food and most medicines, and you could boil water, and building shelter wasn't so much complicated as time consuming, but when it came to defense? Nothing really beat a gun.

And there were only so many guns and bullets.

Sure, new ones were indeed being made, but it was hard. Very hard. It required time and resources and access to the right equipment and knowledge on how to run it. He hadn't run into many gunsmiths.

As they set to work, he looked across one of the outer cabins and something abruptly occurred to him. He walked over to Cait and helped her with her search.

"Babe, you checked on everyone?" he asked.

"Yes," she replied.

"What about those two new girls? The ones we found here?"

"Chloe and Lena. They're still in the cabin we set them up in. Lena was still passed out and Chloe looked wary and frazzled, but she was polite enough when she came to the door. We spoke briefly and according to her, Lena really wants to stick around for a while longer, so if we're okay with it, then they're going to hang out at least through the end of winter. *Are* we okay with that?" she asked, looking at him.

"I'm okay with it, yeah. I'd be surprised if Evie and April wouldn't be," he replied.

Cait smirked suddenly. "I think you have ulterior motives for being okay with it."

"What's that supposed to mean?" he replied, looking up from the desk drawer he was slowly poking through.

"Duh. You want to stick your cock in them."

"I mean...they're both hot. Chloe's hot, Lena's cute," he replied. "But believe it or not, *no,* that isn't the *only* reason, or even the main reason, I want them around."

"Okay, why do you want them around?"

He sighed. "They seem like they've been through a hell of a lot, and they seem nice. I mean, Chloe seemed...aggressive, but it wasn't like she didn't have reason to be. But it's brutal out there, and it seems like they've had to deal with so much, and I just want to give them a place to rest and catch their breath and maybe even find some happiness."

"You are *so* sweet, you know that?"

He sighed. "Lara said the same thing when she saw me petting Frostbite." Cait gasped violently and dropped something. "What?!" he asked, whirling around.

"You *pet* Frostbite?!" she demanded.

He let out his breath as he realized she hadn't seen something dangerous or accidentally hurt herself. "Yes," he replied, "I pet Frostbite. He crawled into my hand and ate some sausage and I petted him for a little bit."

"Oh my fucking God, David. I *need* to see this happen."

He laughed. "Is it really that big of a deal?"

"Yes! Frostbite is fucking *adorable.* Seeing you pet his tiny little mouse head would be the greatest thing ever," she replied with surprising tenacity.

"Okay, okay," he replied, "I'll try and make it happen again. You could probably do it. He'd probably respond to you even better than me, given how motherly you are."

Cait laughed. *"Motherly?* Why, because I'm pregnant?"

"No. Because you're...you know, kind, nurturing, patient."

"I think I'm more of a hot, horny slut than those things," she said.

"...well, moms are hot."

She laughed again. "Yes, they are. Speaking of which, you're going to need to get your hands on some birth control if you want to ride bareback with Amanda. She isn't fixed."

"Shit, that's right. Goddamnit, that's going to be a pain..."

"I'm almost positive the doctors will have some."

"Yeah. Although does it matter? I'm still dubious that she'll actually jump me."

"David. She'll jump you. Trust me. You should pay them a visit today or tomorrow for that birth control," Cait replied.

"All right."

They searched a few minutes more before Cait spoke up again. "What have you got against being cute?" she asked.

"What?"

"You got all defensive when I said it earlier."

"Isn't it obvious?" he replied.

"Maybe, but tell me anyway."

He sighed, considered how best to put it. "Men aren't cute," he said finally. "At least not the ones that other people listen to. Not the ones that inspire confidence, give orders, and run communities. Does that make sense?"

She stopped searching and turned to look at him, an expression of great deliberation on her face. "I'm going to tell you this now, David," she said, "because you've clearly learned this, and it can be very hard to unlearn something. But I'm hoping this plants the seed. What's tougher than a 'tough guy', is a confident guy who gets caught playing with a cute little mouse and called out by some moron with insecurity issues, and responds with, 'Yeah, and?' I know it's going to be hard, and it's going to take time, but you need to learn not to let what people say, or even what you think that they think, bother you. And I understand that you are a leader now, you and I and Evie, we're leaders of this community. So I understand about image, giving people hope, but trust me, David. You want to be the kind of leader that people feel like they can come to with problems, not the kind of leader they're intimidated by and afraid of."

He considered her words for a few moments. "I'm not necessarily disagreeing with you, but which one of those leaders are more likely to triumph in wartime?"

She laughed. "David, you can pet mice *and* kick ass. You've proven that already. What about me? Do you think I should have to choose between being a promiscuous, sexual woman, or an ass-kicking woman? Should I have to choose between being a mother and being a warrior? I can be both. Life isn't that simple, David. It's not either-or. I'm not necessarily saying that you expose your heart to everyone, but...let them know you *have* a heart."

"That makes a lot of sense, actually," he murmured. "Thank you, Cait," he said, stepping closer to her, "for helping me with things like this, for putting up with me."

She smiled and hugged him. "It's not a burden, David. I love you. I want to see you happy. I want to see you better yourself. You're doing great so far. And believe me, I know how hard it is to unlearn certain internal narratives and tendencies."

He nodded. He knew about her past, about growing up under racist parents, picking up those tendencies herself, being forced to confront that aspect of herself, and carve it out like a malignant tumor.

If she had never told him, he'd have never known. They went back to searching after that, and he ruminated on her words.

CHAPTER TWO

They spent a solid five hours there at the camp, first searching the outer perimeter buildings and stripping them of anything useful, then searching and removing all the bodies, dumping them into a pile in a natural divot in the land not too far away.

Most of the zombies had nothing on them, but sometimes they'd find something in one of their pockets, and occasionally it was even useful. They tracked down a ton of weapons in the snow, which was a big pain.

They also went ahead and cleared out the shack that Vanessa and Jennifer had used as cover, though there wasn't much of anything in there. Eventually, as they came to search the central structure, they decided it would be a good time to head home, check in, and drop off their haul.

So, Cait and Ashley remained behind to both guard what was left and continue their search, while David, Evelyn, and Jennifer headed back, hauling as much as they could. Evelyn ended up carrying by far the most weight, given her raw strength, but David found himself loaded down with an overstuffed backpack and a pair of duffel-bags.

As he walked, he kept thinking there would be some kind of conversation between himself and Evie, but she remained silent. Although he at least wasn't getting an angry silence vibe from her, or a sad, sullen silence. Maybe she wasn't ready to talk about the pregnancy? Or maybe she wanted to talk about it alone?

Though he felt like Jennifer was becoming part of the group. Or, at the very least, she was growing very attached to him.

Though she looked pretty unhappy this morning, and she hadn't said much.

As they crossed the bridge over the river, David suddenly put two and two together and felt like an idiot. "Jennifer," he said.

"Yeah?" she asked, sounding a little startled, like she'd been deep in thought.

"Are you doing okay?"

"I..." she hesitated, then looked from him to Evelyn, then sighed. "Not really."

"You want to talk about it?" he asked.

"I don't know if talking will help, but I guess so. It's Ellie. She just...left. I know she was close with Cait, and obviously she was getting really close with you. She was my friend. For a long time, she was the only friend I had in this area. And she just...left. I mean, it's not like we were married or anything, and she didn't shy away from telling me that something like this might happen. She might die because of how dangerous her lifestyle is, or she might decide to move on one day. I just...I guess I thought it wouldn't happen, or there'd be more warning. I feel so blindsided by it."

"I do, too," David murmured.

"I miss her. I mean...did she really say she wasn't coming back?"

"Not...precisely. She said she didn't know when or if she was coming back, and we shouldn't expect her back. I think even she didn't know if she was coming back in that moment."

"Why did she panic? I mean, obviously it had to do with the pregnancy. But I'm not sure why'd she just freak the fuck out and run like that."

"I don't either. I think at this point all we can do

is just hope that she comes back. At the very least I hope she gives us a proper goodbye." He glanced at Evie. "What do you think?"

"I think...she'll be back. I don't know why, it's just what my gut tells me. But I think she needs to sort some things out on her own. And that we should let her."

"Yeah," he and Jennifer murmured.

They didn't say anything for the rest of the walk back, and put down a few zombies that came onto their path, pausing to search their pockets and finding nothing of any significant interest. When they made it back, they found Amanda talking with a woman who had just the previous night threatened him with a knife. Chloe. A third woman was approaching them, which he recognized as the other woman they'd found at the hunting encampment last night, Lena. As they approached, he studied both women.

They seemed a bit of a study in contrasts.

Chloe was little, perhaps a few inches over five feet. She was thin and wiry, with a severe and short haircut, her hair bright blonde. Her skin was tanned and she had a lot of tattoos. One whole arm was a sleeve of them. Everything about her spoke of aggression, defiance, anger. Even her eyes, sharp and blue, looked like they were alive with furious light.

Lena, on the other hand, was almost as tall as he was, and very curvaceous. She was beautiful in a more traditional way, her shoulder-length black hair down, framing her pale face. She had big, green eyes. She had a willowy look to her, and her skin was smooth and pale. Her movements were cautious, hesitant, maybe a little anxious.

Amanda's eyes lit up briefly as she saw him, and she said something quietly to Chloe, who turned around and spotted them. She marched over to them.

They came to a stop before her.

"So, you're the ones in charge, huh?" she asked.

"Not me," Jennifer murmured, taking a step back.

"We're two of the people in charge, yes," David replied.

"Good. One of your people was by to talk to us. A redhead."

"Cait," Evelyn said.

"Yeah. She said we could stay through the end of winter. Is that true?"

David glanced over as the other woman, Lena, came silently up behind Chloe. She stood beside her and a little back, remaining quiet. "That's true," David said. "You can stay here through winter and, if you like, longer."

"So what's the catch then?" Chloe asked. Demanded, was more like it.

"Well, not really what I'd call a catch so much as fair play. We're good so long as neither of you are causing problems. You know, don't steal, don't assault anyone, don't be a loud, obnoxious asshole at four in the morning. The other thing is pull your own weight, which we can negotiate on. Basically, we have a lot of jobs that need doing, and we'd like to find the ones that suit you best, or at the very least you feel comfortable doing. And work hours and changing job positions are negotiable," David explained.

"What kind of jobs?" Chloe asked suspiciously.

"Woodcutting, guard duty, babysitting, snow melting. We're going to have fish traps and rabbit snares soon, so checking those. Hunting game, picking edible plants. Basic 'keep the community running' jobs," David replied.

Chloe stared at him a few seconds longer, her arms crossed, her stance and gaze still challenging, like she expected him to, at any second, demand that she drop to her knees and suck his cock right there in the middle of everyone, and she was almost relishing it, hoping it would happen, just so she could tell him to go to hell and march away.

Finally, she glanced back at Lena, who, he realized, had actually been staring intently at him. When he looked at her, she looked away, down at Chloe, who sighed heavily. "Well?" she asked.

"Yes," Lena replied softly.

Chloe looked back at him. "Okay. We agree to these terms. We'll stay here until the end of winter, then reassess, or until you piss me off."

"Well...I hope it won't be a short stay for you then," David replied, then immediately felt bad for saying it. Evelyn laughed softly, though.

Chloe tensed, but Lena laughed too, actually. "Maybe you being pissed off shouldn't be a condition, babe," she said quietly. "Or we'll have to leave by like tomorrow morning."

"Oh shut up, Lena," she snapped, though with no real venom. She turned around. "And go back to bed. You need to rest. That's what the doctor said."

"They said you need to rest, too," Lena protested.

"I'll be fine. I'm going to bounce off the fucking walls anyway. And I didn't have any real wounds. Just a few scrapes and bruises. Now *go,* Lena."

Lena sighed heavily, then leaned down and kissed her. "Okay. Fine. Please be careful." She looked around. "It was really nice meeting you, and *thank you* for saving our lives." She looked down at Chloe when she put the emphasis on 'thank you'.

Chloe just sighed and rolled her eyes. Lena headed back to their cabin.

Chloe looked at their gear. "Is that from the place we met?"

"Yeah," Evelyn replied.

"You going back?"

"Yes," David said.

"Good, I want to come. I want to help." David and Evelyn hesitated, glancing at each other, but Chloe saved them the trouble. "Look, I know I look like a scrawny little bitch, but I can handle myself, and I can help, and there's something I want to look for back there anyway."

"All right," David said. "Let us drop this stuff off and we'll head back."

As they headed inside, he nodded to Amanda. "Hi," he murmured.

"Hello, David. Make sure to come see me tomorrow tonight, okay? I've got something I *really* want to talk to you about," she replied.

"Uh...yeah. Okay. I'll definitely come find you," he said.

"Good."

They headed into the main office.

"You two fucking? I could've sworn I saw a ring on her finger, and you obviously haven't got one..." Chloe asked.

"No, we're not fucking," David replied.

"Yet," Evelyn murmured. He sighed.

"Okay...so what's the story? The way you two act around each other, I feel like you're together. But I also saw you with the redhead. I *know* I saw you kiss her last night at some point, after we got here."

"Evelyn, Cait, and I, and another woman you may have met, April, the rep who lives in this building, are in an open relationship together," David replied as he set down the duffel-bags with tremendous relief.

"Holy shit, really? Goddamn," Chloe muttered. She looked at Jennifer. "How do you fit into all this?" she asked.

"Me? I, uh, I'm a friend. I live out in the woods. They asked for my help, so I'm here helping," Jennifer replied, setting her own haul down on a table. Evelyn set hers down with a heavy thump on the floor beside it.

"Friends, huh? How close of friends?" she asked, looking between David and Jennifer.

"That's rather...forward," Jennifer murmured.

"Don't answer if you don't want to." She paused. "Sorry. If Lena was here, she'd be aghast and yelling at me to stop being such a nosy bitch. I just like knowing things and I have very little filter between my brain and my mouth. And I think the two of you are *really* good friends, which means that *you,*" she said, pointing at David, "are a fucking wild card."

"What?" he asked.

"Do you know how many human dudes I've run into that would admit to even *wanting* to fuck an inhuman? A jag or a rep, maybe. But a goliath? A wraith? Never." She had a sly smirk on her face, but she lost it suddenly. "Oh fuck, that could come out wrong. I'm sorry. I–to be clear, I'm very sex-positive, interspecies-positive, okay? I'm not making fun of you or talking down to you or anything. I think it's cool. Just...rare. Shit. I should've kept my mouth shut..." she muttered.

"It's fine," Jennifer said. She looked at David, raising her eyebrows a little. He thought he knew what she was asking, so he just nodded. "Yes, David and I are...*close* friends. And, I mean, I get it. I know, it's weird to think about a human fucking a wraith. No one wants to fuck a wraith..."

"Oh, hey, no, come on," Chloe said. She sighed. "Goddamnit, I'm such an idiot. Jennifer, that isn't what I meant. I mean, not exactly...shit." She paused, staring at Jennifer. David held back, wanting to see how exactly this played out. Chloe reminded him a lot of Ellie, which hit him with a pang of sadness. "If it helps, *I'd* totally do you," she said finally.

"Seriously?" Jennifer asked.

"Yes! I'm really into girls, and I've done it with wraiths before, and Lena and I have a...flexible relationship. If you're interested, I'd be happy to apologize with my tongue," Chloe said, grinning a little now.

"I...oh wow," Jennifer murmured. "I...need some time to think about that."

"We should get back to work," David said, diplomatically.

"Yeah, come on, let's go," Chloe agreed, heading for the door.

He took a moment to track down April, who was sorting through supplies upstairs. He checked in with her, updated her on all the new gear that was now downstairs, then gave her a hug and a kiss, and they were off once more.

...

"So...David," Chloe said as they walked back to the hunting grounds area.

"Yeah?" he asked.

"I'm sorry."

He glanced at her. She wasn't looking at him. If

anything, she was specifically looking away from him. "For what?" he asked.

"Threatening your life and being such a bitch with that knife last night. That wasn't fair. You've been nice to us." He saw her tense up, as if bracing herself for her apology to be thrown back into her face, or maybe for him to take advantage of the momentary lowering of armor.

"I accept your apology," he replied. "And I understand. It was an extremely stressful situation. I'm not angry. I'm just glad it worked out as well as it did."

"...okay, good," she murmured. She still seemed tense. He wondered if there was anything he could say to chill her out a little more, to let her know that his group of people was different from probably a lot of others. He really did fully intend to make good on everything he said, and he had no intent to use or manipulate her or Lena in any way. But what could he say that didn't come off as sounding like bullshit? He was sure they'd heard it all before. Ultimately, he knew that all he really had of any real value were his actions.

So he would act accordingly. The only way to build trust was to do the right thing, repeatedly, over the course of time.

That would be easy, at least.

"How'd you end up there?" Jennifer asked.

"At the camp? Fuck. Lena and I have been traveling for a while, looking for a place to settle down for a bit. But we weren't finding anything. We'd had a run of bad luck for a few weeks, and this was just the cherry on the shit cake. We found the place and I didn't want to get involved, but we were pretty desperate. We *needed* a place to get warm, and we were basically out of food and medicine.

"When we tried to negotiate, they basically coerced us into sticking around. We were there for two days, looking for an opportunity to escape. And then you showed up. Luckily none of the filthy fuckers stuck their cocks in us, though they clearly wanted to. I think they were arguing over who got us first. Thank fuck for that," she muttered. "Why did you attack them, anyway? I mean, they deserved it, but what made you do it? Obviously it was a big plan."

"There's a settlement nearby," David replied. "Or there was. They burned it to the ground a few weeks ago, killed dozens of people. And they've caused other problems since then. Saved one woman from them at one point, and they've directly assaulted our base a few times. They're assholes. And now they're dead."

"Now they're all dead," Chloe agreed happily.

They reached the encampment shortly after that and found Cait and Ashley chatting amiably, still hard at work hunting through the main lodge.

"Hey! You're looking better," Cait said as she spied Chloe.

Chloe actually seemed to balk under her gaze, blushing. "Yeah, I, uh, do better when I've actually got something to do," she replied, then laughed nervously and ran a hand through her short hair. David tried not to laugh. He actually got it. Chloe had said she was very into girls, and Cait was the kind of woman who was *intimidatingly* attractive.

"Everything good at home?" Cait asked, glancing at him and Evie.

"Yep," Evie replied.

"Cool! Let's get on with it then," she said, and

resumed working.

They all dove in, hunting for more supplies to haul home.

...

"Hey, whatever happened to that soldier chick?" Chloe asked suddenly.

They were most of the way home now, making what would be their third, and final, trek back. Twilight was gone and now it was dark, the stars coming out. They had, as far as they were concerned, cleaned the place out, taking everything but the furniture, the trash, and the bodies. It had been a pretty decent haul.

There was an okay stash of foods and medicine, and a random assortment of other useful items, like some sewing kits, a pair of binoculars, a few lighters, things like that, but mainly the haul was good for guns. Even though a lot of the guns were in shit shape or even outright broken, there was still a lot of ammo, and even a broken gun had its uses.

"Lara? She had to go back to her unit," David replied.

"Unit? Like a real military unit? I didn't think they existed anymore," Chloe said.

"They don't. I mean, as far as I know. It's a group of people made up of some people who are ex-military, and they operate like a military unit, with ranks and uniforms and shit like that."

"Why the *fuck* weren't *they* helping us? Or was there more I wasn't seeing?"

"No. Lara was the only one, and she had to disobey orders to do so," Evie said.

"What the *fuck!?* Why!?" Chloe demanded.

"Their leader has a stick up his ass and pretty much said those assholes weren't important enough. Thankfully, Lara managed to slip out."

"Fucking bullshit," she muttered, then she yawned. "Goddamn I'm so tired. I'm going to go find Lena and get some food and then sleep."

"All right." Cait and Evie accepted the bags she was carrying, as they'd given her a lighter load. "Thanks for your help, it was really appreciated," Cait said.

"Uh...yeah. Not a problem." She turned and hurried off towards their cabin.

"Wow, she *really* likes you, huh?" Evie murmured.

"Oh yeah. She likes me so much she doesn't know how to handle it," Cait replied.

"You think that was a real offer? Or was she just being polite?" Jennifer asked.

"I think Chloe isn't nice enough to go down on someone just because it'd be polite. I think it was a real offer," David replied.

"I hope so. She's really hot," Jennifer murmured.

"Yep," David agreed, and he heard murmurs of assent from the other three women as well.

They walked into the main building and began setting down the gear they'd collected. David let out a long sigh of relief as he set down the backpack and bag full of guns he'd been carrying. Guns were fucking heavy.

"Well, I apparently *need* to go spend time with my family," Ashley said. There was something in her voice, something that had been off about her all day that David had been picking up on. But between his new, full realization of his responsibility, Cait's pregnancy, and getting the job done today, he hadn't really been able to focus much on it.

Now he did, and it immediately became apparent what was wrong: Ellie. Yet another person who Ellie had connected with that she had apparently abandoned. Fuck, this just kept sucking more and more.

"They miss you," Evie said. "Try not to hold it against them."

She sighed. "Yeah, that's fair. Well, goodnight all. I'll see you tomorrow."

They told her goodnight and she headed out.

"Let's get this shit secured and we can deal with it after dinner," David said.

"Good idea. Why don't you and Cait get started on dinner, and Jennifer can help me haul this stuff upstairs?" Evie suggested.

"Fine by me," Cait said. "Come on, dear."

He followed happily after her.

The next hour passed fairly blissfully as he and Cait prepared a large dinner of cooked venison, some vegetable stew, and some baked potatoes. They'd been eating well lately, but that was the benefit of working with a farmstead. Although this was going to have to calm down, and meals were likely going to have to become more conservative again if they were going to store food in a real capacity.

Once they got the meal made, they served it and Jennifer, Evelyn, and April joined them at the table. As they dug in, David found his mind coming back around to the future. The immediate future. It was something he couldn't escape for long.

There was still *so* much to do.

Not long after he'd finished, he excused himself and then went to track down the map they had been keeping of the region. Everyone added to it what they could. He also grabbed the notebook Evelyn was using to keep track of things and brought both back to the table.

"It's time to get serious again," he said, setting them both down. "I've been thinking about our goal now."

"What is our goal, precisely?" Cait asked.

"To turn this place into an actual, sustainable settlement, as self-reliant as possible," he replied. "Which means we need a few things. We need to make repairs and, if possible, upgrades to the perimeter fence. We'll also need materials to make repairs to the cabins. Some of them have broken windows, some have holes in the roof, or the walls. We're going to need, at the very least, a big, huge store of food. Water we can do for ourselves. Ideally, I'd like to find a hydroponic garden. I don't think we'd be able to grow enough to sustain *everyone,* but anything to ease the day-to-day burden would be a great idea," David explained.

"What else?" Jennifer asked.

"Medicine. We need a big supply of medicine," April said. "Antibiotics, painkillers, gauze, bandages, basically anything we can get our hands on. The more the merrier."

"Excellent. So: a stock of building materials, a stock of food, a stock of water, a stock of medicine, and a stock of guns. Which I feel like we have pretty secured right now." He looked at Evelyn. "Make a list, with bullet points under each one. Under food, we'll need both a big amount of food stocked and the hydroponic garden."

"Yep," she agreed, grabbing a pen and flipping to a new page.

"Anything else?" he asked.

"We'll want a generator," Cait said. "Not exactly *need* per se, but it would go a long way towards making this place feel more like a home."

He nodded. "So, where do we get all this stuff? There's abandoned buildings all over the place, but they'll have mostly been cleared out..."

"There's that construction site," Cait said. "The abandoned one in the valley."

David nodded. He remembered when they'd passed it on the way to the thieves' hideout, him and Ellie, when they'd first done that recon. "Yeah, there could be some supplies there. Anywhere else?" he asked.

Cait sighed. "I mean...there's a lot of places. Like the abandoned farmhouse, the railway center, a ton of cabins and houses dotting the landscape, but they're all cleared out at this point. We might end up having to trade for it."

"Wait," David said, leaning forward suddenly, "the warehouse. That warehouse I investigated and got jumped by some wildcats in a while ago. There were crates in there. A lot of them. They might be empty or full of useless junk, but they might not. We never went back."

Cait nodded. "Yeah, that *is* dangerous territory. It would keep most people away, and if there was still stuff there...it *was* on my list of places to someday raid for supplies. All right, so we've got two places, but that will probably turn up construction related stuff, and *maybe* a generator. What about the rest of it?"

"The bunker," Jennifer said suddenly.

"The what?" April asked.

"There's a bunker, out in the middle of nowhere," Jennifer said.

David nodded. "Yeah, remember when I told you that Cait, Ellie, and I got attacked by like two hundred stalkers, and the military team showed up and saved, and then robbed, us? It was at a bunker in the forest. But...I thought it was locked."

"It is," Cait said. "Locked down *tight*."

"I think I can get in," Jennifer said.

"And you never mentioned this?" Cait asked.

"No, I didn't, because it's a bit of a long shot, and because I have trust issues."

"Okay, that's fair." Cait looked at David, who looked back at her, then shifted his gaze over to Jennifer.

"What will you need?" he asked.

"There's a tool I have. Although I do need another, closer look at the lock."

"All right. We'll put it on the list." He fell silent for a moment, considering it. "So this is it? Three places?" he asked.

"For now," Cait replied. "I'll see what else I can come up with. Plus, we can hit up Vanessa and Katya. They're also explorers, when they can be. So they might know of a few places. And before you ask, I would say that yes, we can trust them. The doctors are paranoid, but they have right to be. Vanessa and Katya are more reasonable, and we have an understanding. I think this is a great starting place, though. We can get started tomorrow."

David nodded and yawned. "Yeah. I think we should hit up the warehouse first, it's the closest and I'm super curious as to what's in those crates."

"All right, we'll do it tomorrow. In the meantime..." She sighed. "I guess we should get to work organizing all that stuff we found. We'll definitely need your help," she said, looking at

Jennifer, "if you're cool to stick around a while longer."

"Yeah, I don't mind," Jennifer replied.

"Great! Well, come on, let's go sort through guns for the rest of the night," Cait said, and got up.

David stood and they started to clean off the table.

CHAPTER THREE

David knocked on April's door.

It was cracked and flickering light came from beyond it. "Come in," she said.

He pushed the door open and found her laying in bed. They'd sorted all the guns out over the course of the next four hours, and had begun the process of stripping apart the broken ones, seeing what spare parts they could salvage.

Finally, they'd all headed for bed. Jennifer had, in an adorably hesitant way, asked Cait if she could sleep in her bed tonight, to which Cait had happily responded yes, so they were there now, and he could hear them beneath the floor he was now standing on, occasionally moaning.

April set aside the book she was reading and stared at him intently. She looked worried. David closed the door behind him and crossed the room, sitting down on the bed beside her. He had considered how to tackle this, or even if he should yet. But it felt wrong not to. He didn't want to feel like he was keeping anything from any of them, and in his experience, when you had a problem, the sooner you could face it, the better.

"I thought we should talk, about the development with Cait," he said.

"Okay," she replied, and he thought she sounded cautious.

He reached out and took her hand. "This isn't anything bad, April. I mean...did you think it was going to be?" he asked.

"I thought...maybe..." she hesitated, looked away.

"Whatever it is, you can tell me. I want to be

clear that nothing's changed about how *I* feel about *you*. If anything, it's only gotten better," he replied.

She looked back at him, and for a moment seemed to be deciding whether or not she could fully believe him, then she adopted a tentative smile. "I was just worried that, with Cait pregnant, you were going to tell me that you would have to shift focus to her. Which, I mean, would be fair. I just thought you might not have time for me anymore."

"April," he said, and then he hugged her. She hugged him very tightly back.

"I'm sorry," she said, before he could continue. "I'm sorry. I know I'm annoying, and anxious, and I get worked up over things. I'm trying not to. I know you said I should worry less, but it's just so hard sometimes."

"It's okay," he replied, rubbing one hand up and down her back. "It's okay, April. I'm not mad or annoyed. I get that you have issues, and they aren't going to just go away. I want to help you, and I understand that sometimes, being helpful is being patient, and moving at the pace that you most feel comfortable with."

"That's...so very understanding," she said. "I feel like I don't deserve that."

"You do," he replied, and gave her a little squeeze. She squeezed him back hard.

"Okay," she whispered. They sat like that for a moment longer, then she pulled back. She had a smile on her face, and some tears in her eyes. She brushed them away. "I'm actually excited about the kid. I can help Cait, because I actually know about pregnancy. Things to watch for, ways to help deal with the side effects, even some child care stuff."

"I would love for you to be involved, and I'm

positive Cait will, too," he replied, which made her smile more broadly. Then he hesitated. "There's one other thing."

"What?" she asked, losing her smile.

He laughed softly. "It's not bad! I mean, I think. I don't know how you'll react. I think it's good." He paused again. She stared at him, waiting. "I told Cait that I loved her, and she says that she loves me," he said.

"Okay...that makes sense," she murmured, waiting for the other shoe to drop again.

"And when I realized that I love her, and what that feels like, it made me realize that...I love you, too," he said.

"...oh," she said softly, and the small smile came back to her. "Oh." Her eyes became a little unfocused and dreamy. He waited patiently for her to process this. He wasn't sure what was going through her mind, but it seemed to be good. After about half a minute, all at once she refocused on him. "Say it again," she said.

"I love you, April," he said.

And she let out a loud laugh and kissed him. "I love you, too, David."

Hearing that.

Hearing those words from her was just...wonderful. And it felt right. Love was something that concerned him, and had for a long time, because it was so vague. People were so...evasive, about it. Like, their answers were something along the lines of 'You'll know it when you feel it', or 'You'll just know'.

Which always bothered the shit out of him. Now, though? If pressed, he could do a better job of explaining it to someone, but he *did* know now. It felt...unique. It didn't really feel like anything else he'd felt before.

"Can we have sex?" she asked suddenly.

"Yes," he replied immediately, and got to his feet. He started taking off his clothes and she took off the t-shirt she was wearing. He watched her reach under the blanket and shift around a bit, probably taking off her panties. As soon as he was naked, she lifted the blankets for him, and he caught sight of her slim, nude body before getting in next to her. That still sent such a thrill of excitement through him.

As he got beneath the blankets with her, David pressed himself against her and they began to kiss. He ran one hand down her side, to her slim hip, then down to her trim thigh, feeling all her smooth, scaly skin.

Then he fitted his hand between her thighs and his fingertip sought her clit.

She gasped in surprised pleasure as they met, then began to moan into the kiss as he started to massage it with slow circular motions.

"Oh my fucking God, *yes,* David..." she moaned. "You are...I can-oh!-I can say this without embellishment, without it being about stroking your ego, you are the *best* guy I have ever been with in bed. I haven't been with many, but you are the *best.* The way you touch me is just so...perfect. It's *so* satisfying."

He grinned and began to go a little harder, a little faster, making her cry out. "The best guy? But not the best overall?"

"No," she whispered, panting. "I'm sorry. You're great, definitely number two, but–"

"But it's Cait, isn't it?" he asked.

She nodded. "Uh-huh...does that bother you?"

"Fuck no. She's absolutely stellar in bed," he replied. "I'm glad she does it for you so well. She *really* likes you."

"She seems to. *Oh fuck!*" she cried in surprise, and then he had her orgasming. She was fucking sensitive and wired tonight. Her whole tight little body writhed and twisted and spasmed as she came and she looked so fucking good when she orgasmed. Almost as soon as she was done, she grabbed him. "Get in me, *please,*" she begged.

"You got it," he replied, already going for the lube.

He found it and got some onto his dick, glad that they had a healthy supply on hand, and then she spread her legs as he got on top of her. She moaned loudly as he penetrated her, and he felt that wonderfully familiar, mind-numbingly good pleasure begin a slow burn into him as he slid inside of her. He buried his whole rigid length in her tight, *tight* inhuman vagina one thrust at a time.

He could feel her moving against him as they started to make love, feel her pressing her hips up against his, forcing him deeper into her, feel the wonderful, scaly smoothness of her bare body against his own. She wrapped her arms around him, staring up at him with wide eyes.

"I love you," she moaned. "I love you so much, David..."

"Oh April," he groaned, kissing her hard on the mouth. "I love you, too."

"Oh *David!*" she screamed as soon as he said that, and then she was coming again. He felt surprised, very pleasantly so, but definitely surprised. April was sensitive, but this seemed to be shoving her into overdrive.

He groaned at the fresh release of her sex juices, the convulsion of her vaginal muscles around his cock, the increased pleasure of feeling her climax. And he kept fucking her, kept stroking smoothly into her again and again.

Her slick, smooth pussy felt so incredibly good against his bare cock. They kissed passionately as they made love, and all throughout this, David was realizing that this, too, was different now. Would it be different with everyone? Or just the women he loved? In either case, this was a very welcome development.

He moaned her name again and again as they made love, and after several more minutes, he grabbed her suddenly and brought them around so that he was on his back and she was now atop him. She reacted to this immediately, and he loved how in tune with each other they were. She rose up and began to ride him, moaning louder.

Beneath them, David could hear Jennifer and Cait making their own sex sounds. David grabbed her hips and helped her ride him, bouncing her on his cock furiously, the pleasure and ecstasy melting into him.

"Please-David, yes! *Don't stop!*" she begged, her high, firm breasts bouncing in sync with her.

He loved it when she was like this, when she was just completely lost in sex, because it seemed that she had no anxieties, that she could escape them. There were times where she would get self-conscious, usually before or after, but in all their most recent sessions, she seemed to trust him and to believe in herself, to just not worry, and he was glad that he was able to do that for her. He hoped it was like this with Cait, with everyone else she hooked up with.

David's orgasm surprised him, seeming to come

out of nowhere a few moments later, bursting into being, and he cried out, feeling his whole body pulse with the pleasure of release as he shot his load into her.

"Mmm...yes, David," she moaned, grinning and grasping his wrists, then bringing his hands up to her breasts, where he immediately began to grope them. "I *love* making you come so much. I love feeling you coming inside of me."

"Oh fuck, April, I love you!" he cried.

"I love you too, David," she moaned, taking his seed into her.

He came inside of her in a glorious, impassioned display of pure ecstasy, his body thrumming with bliss as he climaxed.

When he was finished, he went slack, staring up at her. She smiled down at him, her hands on his bare chest now. "I'm so happy that I have you in my life. I still can't believe it, honestly. I've never had someone be as kind to me as you are, and as Cait and Evie have been. I kind of thought that kindness was a myth, that if someone was being kind to me, it was because they had some ulterior motive. I've never really felt...safe, or loved, not like I do with you and Evie and Cait." She laid down against him and hugged him tightly.

He hugged her back. "I'm so glad you feel safe and loved, April. You deserve it."

They held each other a while longer, and eventually, the knowledge that he had to go talk with Evie about all this drove him from April's bed. He told her why, and she said it was fine. They spent a moment cleaning up together, and when they were done, he dressed and she laid back down. She picked back up the book she'd been reading.

"I love you," she said as he headed out.

"I love you, too, April," he replied, and closed the door to a crack behind him.

He found Evie in their bed, also reading. She was propped up against several pillows, the blankets pulled up around her huge breasts. She smiled at him as she set aside her book. "Hey you," she said.

"Hello, honey," he replied, pulling his clothes off again. He wasn't sure why he'd put them back on. Force of habit, he supposed.

"Sounds like you and April had a nice time."

"Oh yes, we did." He finished undressing and got into bed. "We need to talk."

"I know," she said, and looked at him patiently.

"I'm a little worried," he admitted after a moment of considering it. Evie was always sharp, and he thought she already knew a lot of what he was going to say.

"About your four-way relationship, now that Cait is pregnant?" she asked.

"Yeah. I don't want anyone feeling, you know, neglected. I mean, I have no fucking idea how to be a parent. That alone is scaring me, on top of running a goddamned village, *and* I need to somehow find time for two *other* people in my life," he said, the words tumbling out of him before he could even stop to consider them.

Evie opened her arms. "Come here," she said. He came to her, laid against her, and she hugged him, held him. "It's okay, David. You're scared. That's normal. I'm scared. We're all scared. Of the zombies, the assholes out there, the weather, and our own relationships. I'd say...the fact that you care enough to question yourself, and worry, means you've won half the battle. The rest of it is effort. But you aren't the only one putting in effort, David. We all are. And as for Cait's pregnancy...well, I spoke with Cait about it. She was worried, too. She didn't want to say anything, but she did tell me she feels a little guilty."

"Why?" he asked.

"Well, think about it. She's the last one who joined this relationship, she kind of jumped into it, after April and I were already here, and now she's pregnant, and that's going to take up more of your time, and she didn't want to take you from us. But I'll tell you exactly what I told her, because it made her feel a lot better. One of the most important aspects of our relationship, and by our I mean all of us, is that we share everything.

"We share trust, we share communication, we share sex, we share time and energy. We're going to share raising this child, David. You and me and Cait and April. We're all going to be parents, is the point I'm trying to make."

"And you don't...I guess...I don't know, I mean, it doesn't bother you that you had no say in this? I guess is what I'm asking?" he asked hesitantly.

Evie laughed. "Dear, a lot of pregnancies are surprises. Ideally, they wouldn't be, and that can cause a lot of problems, but think about it. You chose to acknowledge your role as a parent, you chose to step into that role, when you could have walked away, or even chosen to stay, but be less involved, more distant, allowing Cait to take on the role of parent by herself. So I'm choosing to be a parent, too. And I'm sure April will, as well."

"Okay," he murmured.

A moment went by. "David?"

"Yes?"

"I love you," she said. He looked up at her, surprised, momentarily at a loss for words. "You've told the others that, haven't you?"

He nodded. "How'd...you know? Did you hear me?"

"Well...I sure heard you and April saying it when you were having sex just now. But I knew. I could see it in the way you looked at Cait when she told you about the pregnancy. I knew that you had fallen in love with her. And I could tell she had fallen in love with you...a few days ago, I think."

"Seriously?"

"Yeah."

"How could you tell?"

"It's hard to describe. I've just seen it before. There's this look that older couples who are still together and still really happy give each other sometimes. Sometimes at the same time, sometimes when the other isn't looking." She laughed softly. "And you gave it to me recently. That look. I had to think about how I felt about it."

"How do you feel about it...about me loving you?" he asked.

"Good. Great. You're a wonderful man, David. I'm so happy you're in my life, and that we met. And I've had enough time to figure out that I love you, and I love April, and Cait. And that we're all *very* lucky to have found each other, and that I will fight tooth and fucking nail to keep this," she replied.

"I'm luckier," he murmured, and hugged her more tightly to him.

She laughed and hugged him back. "Now, is there anything else?"

"Um...no, I think that about covers it," he replied.

"Good. Then in that case, *I* want *my* turn with you giving me a hard dicking," she said.

He laughed and sat up. "Okay then, spread your

legs."

"Yes, sir."

...

David opened his eyes as he felt the bed shifting around him, then he groaned as he felt a hot hand wrap around his cock, which was hard as hell, and begin to massage. There was lube on it, he realized groggily.

"What's going on? Who's that?" he muttered. There was some light coming in through the windows, but not much. It was probably six or seven in the morning.

"Your pregnant slut," Cait replied. She continued shifting around as he tried to come awake, and the blankets were pulled back, then she got on top of him, facing away. He found himself looking at her big, pale ass. Then she was reaching behind herself and gripping his slicked-up cock. She shifted around until she had it pointed at her ass.

"Oh, *fuck,* Cait!" he moaned loudly as she began lowering her fat ass onto his cock, taking it slowly inside of herself.

"Yep," she replied, sounding very pleased with herself, "that's what I like to hear...mmm...fuck, you're big," she whispered, and started pushing it deeper into herself.

"Oh my fucking God, Cait. That's just...holy fucking...agh!" he moaned, reaching out and gripping her big ass.

"Mmm, yes...just imagine how much hotter this will be when my ass is even fatter from the pregnancy," she murmured.

"Yes..." he groaned as he started thrusting up into

her. She let out a loud cry of pleasure.

It didn't take him long to blow his load, with the feeling of her insanely tight ass clenched around his cock, the way it felt sliding in there again and again, and just the sight of it. The fucking sight of her huge, perfectly shaped, pale ass going up and down, his cock disappearing into it. This early in the morning, it was just too much.

He came so hard, pumping her sweet ass full of his seed.

She let him finish up, then she got off of him and went to go clean herself up. Someone tossed a warm washrag onto his chest.

"Clean up," Evie said. "It's my turn next."

David began to clean up.

Half an hour later, he found himself clean, dressed, fed, and on the road with Evelyn and Cait. They had decided that they'd go and investigate the warehouse while Jennifer, April, and Ashley tended to things at the campgrounds, as a few problems had cropped up overnight. One of the children had gotten sick, so April was helping them out, and there was still a lot of supplies to be sorted from their haul at the hunting lodge, on top of the other regular duties they were still establishing. David found himself wondering how long it was going to take to get through this period of frantic activity and settle back into routine, like during those two weeks of blizzards.

Now, though, he'd actually look forward to that.

At some point, hopefully, it would get quiet, and there would be time.

But that point was not now. He kept his focus up as they walked through the woods, sticking to a path he'd found earlier that would take them to the road the warehouse was built alongside. He remembered the first time he'd found that warehouse. It was where he had met Ellie. He didn't want to think about her.

She was gone, but forever?

Fuck, for all he knew she could be shadowing them right this very second, watching them from afar in cover. She was good enough to do that. David looked around again as they emerged from the trees and came out onto a cracked, snowy road. In the distance, he could see the warehouse.

As they began to draw closer, however, David heard the distinct sound of gunfire, and it seemed to be coming from the warehouse. At the same time, he saw a slim figure race across the street, what he recognized as a wildcat, hit the side of the warehouse, and scramble up it. He shuddered and pulled out his pistol.

The gunfire intensified.

"Someone's in trouble," he said, and began sprinting.

Cait and Evie followed in his wake, their own weapons out. He listened to what sounded like an intense battle raging inside the warehouse and saw several more wildcats begin coming for it from across the street.

As soon as he could, David drew a bead on one of them and opened fire. The first shot missed, but the second nailed one through the leg. That got their attention. Three of them turned to face him and began to race towards him. Cursing, he skidded to a halt, took careful aim, and began squeezing the trigger.

He popped off shots until his pistol ran dry, putting down two of the wily bastards, and Cait managed to kill the third one, while Evie shot two more that emerged from the trees. As they started running again, the front doors to the warehouse suddenly burst open. A man emerged, running blindly forward, facing back and firing a pistol. He was screaming. A second after he emerged, a pack of wildcats came shrieking out after him.

"This way!" David screamed.

The man's head snapped towards him and he changed trajectory in an instant, and he was running towards them. David and the others shifted to the sides, to get a better angle on the pursuing wildcats, and they opened fire again after reloading.

David put a round into one's skull, sending it sprawling to the cold pavement, then shot another twice in the gut and as it was tripped up, fired a bullet into its head, spraying the snow with its brains. Evie and Cait held steady and put down the rest of them, pelting their bodies with lead and turning them into corpses.

The man nearly reached them before skidding to a halt. He raised his pistol suddenly, trembling badly. "W-who are you!?" he demanded.

"Relax. My name's David. This is Evelyn and Cait. We're not going to hurt you," David replied, lowering his own pistol slowly. He studied the man. He had dark skin, a buzzed haircut, some wrinkles around his eyes, and a scar down one cheek. He wore a big, gray coat and faded work pants with hiking boots. He looked like hell.

Finally, he lowered the pistol. "I'm sorry. Can you help? We need help," he said. He looked back. "Fuck, I have to check on them."

He turned and ran off.

They followed. "We can help," David called.

"Thanks!" he called back, and disappeared into the warehouse.

"Cait, will you stay here and make sure nothing

else comes inside?" David asked as they reached the front door. He could hear several voices inside.

"Yeah, babe. Be careful," she replied.

"You too."

He and Evelyn headed inside.

It seemed as though they hadn't been there for very long. Not much was different about the warehouse, though they'd had time to set up at least a basic camp. He saw several bedrolls and sleeping bags gathered around a metal crate where someone had started a fire. Supplies were scattered all over the place and several people were moving about slowly, some of them in a daze. There were a few more laying on the floor.

There were several dead wildcats, and he could see the same broken window from overhead that Ellie had fired through weeks ago to save his ass.

The man from before moved among the survivors, checking them over. Some of them looked at David and Evie warily. They stood by, waiting for the man to return. He wanted to offer help, but honestly, when it came to how people reacted to outsiders, it could be a complete gamble.

Some would welcome help with open arms, some would shoot you in the face just for approaching, and a whole gamut of other possibilities rested between, most of them not pleasant. So, typically speaking, the correct thing to do was wait.

After a few minutes, he did return. He still looked very worried, but more composed. "I'm sorry about earlier, I was panicking. My name is Robert. I'm the leader of this, uh, group. You said you could help us? We need help."

David offered his hand, and Robert shook it. "David," he repeated, in case the man hadn't heard him or had forgotten. It was very easy to do in a tense situation with so much going on. "Yes, we can and will help. What do you need right now?"

"Medical supplies. We have several wounded. We got lucky, none of them seem to have been attacked by wildcats, but we've been traveling for weeks. Some of us are sick. One person has an infection they got from a cut from a bad fall...we don't have any meds left."

"We have a settlement nearby, we can get your people there," David said.

He grimaced and glanced back reluctantly. "Some of them should really be tended to before we move them," he replied, looking forward again.

"We didn't bring hardly any meds with us," Evie muttered.

"I know where we can get some meds," David replied. "Stay here with Cait and help them as best you can. I'll go get us some medical supplies."

"Maybe one of us should go with you..."

"No," he said. "I can be there and back in fifteen, maybe twenty minutes, and the wildcats might attack again. They're bad in this area."

Robert heaved a sigh. "Of course they are. It's one goddamned motherfucking thing after another," he muttered angrily.

"Don't worry, we'll get you help," David said. "I'll be back."

"Thank you," Robert replied.

"Love you, Evie," he said, and gave her a quick kiss, because he really could die out there, and if that was the case, then he wanted the last thing he ever said to her to be that he loved her. He found Cait and updated her.

"Okay, be careful out there," she said, grasping

his hand. "It's not like I didn't give a shit before, but...well, I'm going to need you around more than ever," she said, and placed his hand against her stomach.

"I know. I'll be careful. I'll come back soon. I love you, Cait."

"I love you too, David."

They shared a kiss and then he was off.

CHAPTER FOUR

David was alone again, walking through a frozen forest.

He thought about how he had gotten here as he kept an eye out for undead. He thought about the tragedy in his life, the people he had known who had died, the long, sleepless nights. But mostly he thought about how different he was now.

The person who he had been a little over a month ago when he'd first come into the region seemed so distant. He'd never really been an 'in charge' kind of person. He never gave orders, he never took control, he never oversaw things, other than his own life. And even then a lot of the times it didn't particularly feel like he was an active participant. It more felt like he was just…

Doing things, and drifting along.

He had always wanted, to one degree or another, to be the kind of person he was becoming right now. Someone who was decisive, and brave, and, well, obviously, fucking three different women in a four-way relationship. But he was disappointed in how brave he *didn't* feel right now. He just felt scared.

What if he really did die out here?

What if someone back there died while he was gone?

Fuck, what if Evie or Cait died because that was a trap that he hadn't recognized for what it was? Those people *seemed* on the level, but what if they weren't? Cait and Evie could take care of themselves, but there was only so much you could do when the odds were stacked against you. All of this was just more incentive to hurry up.

Other things plagued him as he walked on. There were a good dozen people there. Would they be interested in living at the campgrounds? Would Evie and Cait be okay with it? David wanted to help them, and they had the room, but that was more resources, and they knew nothing about these people.

He supposed that was how settlements went. Typically speaking, you were innocent until proven guilty. You could come in and live until you fucked up. That was a fair policy, and ultimately the one he wanted to adopt, but still...

He couldn't help but be paranoid.

But this was his life now. He was going to help people. David wanted to become the kind of person that chose to help people, and managed to do it effectively. Right now, that meant tracking down medicine.

Not but a few minutes later, he spied the watchtower that he had first made love with Ellie in. He ignored the bad feelings that began to infect him as he ascended the tower, keeping wary of anything that might be lurking. He got to the top of the watchtower and hesitated. The front door was hanging open.

Peering in through the windows, he could tell immediately that someone had been by, and he very much doubted it was Ellie. The place looked tossed. Drawers were pulled open and, in some cases, just out and dumped on the floor. Random items were scattered across the floor. The bed he'd slept on, had sex with Ellie on, was tipped over.

David sighed softly and headed inside. He wasted five minutes poking through the interior, managing to find a single magazine of ammo, a few books, and some cans of food that he slipped into his pack.

So, time for Plan B.

He headed back down to the ground and struck off southbound, remembering the little cave that Ellie had pointed him towards. As he walked, he suddenly wondered if it *was* Ellie who had tossed the watchtower.

She'd left in such a state, basically a panic, that he could imagine her coming here and grabbing whatever she could find. He wanted to find her, even though he knew she needed to be on her own. He wanted just to help her–

"Fuck!"

Something crashed into him from his right and suddenly David found himself on his back with a stalker shrieking in his face. David screamed back as panic ignited his body and he fought furiously to get it off of him. In a surge of strength, he threw it off of him while rolling to the right. The second it was free of him, he managed to grab his knife and rip it free of its sheath.

He brought it up just as the thing scrambled for him again, coming at him on all fours, and shoved the blade into its eye. The stalker began to shriek again and then the sound abruptly cut off as it went slack. For several seconds, David just laid there on the snowy ground, panting, shaking violently as adrenaline screamed through him. Then he heard a groan nearby.

"Fuck," he whispered, and pulled the blade out, then got quickly to his feet.

Should've had his fucking gun out, he thought angrily as he wiped off the blade and slipped it back into the sheath. He pulled out his pistol as he started making his way through the trees once more, his pace a bit more clipped this time around. Then again, if he had, it probably would've just flown out of his hands. That thing had been waiting for him behind a big tree. Goddamnit! That had scared the absolute fucking shit out of him.

David began to worry as he pressed forward, hearing several zombies moving about nearby, drawn in by his shouting. He'd like to get in and out with as little conflict as possible, but he was a little hazy on the location of the cave. There was the cliff face up ahead, he could see it through the trees, but where was the cave?

Had he passed it already? He didn't think so, but all of this shit looked the same.

The zombies were getting closer. Or were they? It was so hard to tell in this fucking forest. He hesitated, glancing back. Maybe he should head back...

He looked forward again, frowned and squinted, then moved a few more steps closer.

There it was!

With a sigh of relief, David hurried towards the cave.

. . .

David didn't feel any relief until he was actually back inside of the warehouse and could see Cait and Evelyn still alive and okay. He was glad to see that the situation seemed to have improved a little bit since he'd come back. Everything was calmer, and the people had organized their belongings a bit more, probably preparing to leave. He wondered what kind of discussion they'd had with Evie and Cait so far.

Evelyn came over to him as she saw him

approaching.

"Got the meds," he said, shrugging out of his pack and dropping down into a crouch to zip it open and fish them out.

"Good. Things aren't terrible, but they're clearly shaken. Cait and I have spoken about it and we're willing to offer them a place to stay at the campgrounds. How do you feel about it?" she asked, crouching beside him.

"I'm fine with it," he replied. "Although it's gonna get a little tight. At least until we repair some of the shittier cabins. Some of them aren't in a state to be lived in, not during winter...here," he said, passing her the meds.

"Okay, I'll get them passed around. The people here seem like good people, so far. They've definitely had it rough. You should talk with Robert."

"I will," he replied.

Evelyn headed off, back towards the group. David looked at Robert and tilted his head to the right, then moved over to the door. A moment later, the two men were standing outside.

"Before anything else: thank you for the help. If you don't fuck us over, you're the first helpful person we've seen in a long time," Robert said.

"You're welcome, and I understand. I'd say 'don't worry, we're not going to fuck you over', but I imagine you've heard something to that tune before."

Robert laughed bitterly, his breath foaming on the air.

"So you're the one in charge?" he asked.

"No. All three of us are. Inasmuch as anyone's in charge at the settlement. Evelyn said that she and Cait offered to let you stay?"

"Yeah. Contingent on your say so, and we're

ready to find a place to settle down. At the very *least* we would like a place to just park ourselves for the winter."

"Understood. I'm okay with it. There's a few ground rules: everyone contributes, don't cause problems, and we're a mixed group. Humans and jags and reps and goliaths welcome. Honestly, anyone's welcome as long as they don't cause problems. I also know how some people are about wraiths, so I'm going to say that we are friends with a wraith and she is presently back at the settlement, helping out."

"That's fine," Robert replied. "I don't have a problem with inhumans. As far as I know, no one in my group does either. And that's fair, we don't mind working. But I swear to God if you're running a labor camp..."

"No, no, it's nothing like that," David said. "I mean, you'll see it when you get there, but anyone's free to leave whenever they want. And the jobs and working hours are negotiable. If someone's sick, we're not going to drag them out of bed and force them to chop wood for ten hours. Honestly, I just want a happy, safe community."

Robert looked at him for a moment, as if judging him, then sighed. "I'm sorry, that was rude of me. It's just...been a long winter."

"What happened?" he asked. "If don't mind talking about it?"

He groaned and rubbed his eyes. "Where to begin? We're all from the same settlement. It's like eighty miles away from here, or something. Shit, could be more, I don't know at this point. Anyway, we got attacked by this *huge* pack of stalkers. We're talking hundreds. It was awful. They were everywhere. We ran, regrouped, kept running. After that, it was a long, long search for a new place to live.

"Found one place that turned out to be run by this military asshole who was pretty much a dictator, running a forced labor camp. Another place was pretty much run by this gang of assholes who just did whatever they wanted. Several places just weren't big enough for us to stay at and we mostly wanted to stay together..."

He sighed heavily and rubbed his eyes again, then reached into his pocket and pulled out a cigarette. "You smoke?"

"No thanks, I'm good."

"Okay." He lit up and took a long pull on it. "Fuck. Not enough of these left. Anyway, we've just been rolling pretty much. Looking for a place to stay. We've died or just stayed behind at one of the smaller villages in ones and twos, and now there's just twelve of us left. Do you have enough room for all of us?"

"Yeah, right now we do. We've got cabins. They're not in the *best* condition, but we're actively working to fix them up. We, too, experienced a great tragedy when someone burned down the village we were living in a month ago."

"Oh shit, that sucks. Are they still around?"

"No, we killed them recently, actually. Day before last. They'd been harassing everyone for the past month or two, and we finally decided enough was enough."

"Well, damn. That puts you up above most community leaders I've met. If you're really on the level, you seem like a decent guy *and* a decisive one. Most people in that situation just kind of roll over and do whatever the bullies want."

"Well, to be fair, attacking does come with its own risks and drawbacks. And it wasn't just me. I had a lot of help," David replied. He shivered as a particularly cold gust of wind cut through the area. Robert did as well and stubbed out his cigarette on the side of the building.

"Shit, it's cold. I guess we should probably get going."

The headed back into the warehouse.

"If your people are ready, yes. Our camp is maybe a fifteen or twenty minute walk from here, in the woods," David replied. "Although there *is* one thing I'd like help with."

"Name it," Robert replied.

"Did you look through these crates?" he asked, indicating the stacks of crates that took up an appreciable portion of the warehouse.

"No, we didn't have the time or energy," he replied.

"Okay. I need to look through at least some of them, and if there's anything worthwhile, I'd like help hauling it back," David said.

He nodded. "Yeah, definitely. I've got a prybar, let me go get it."

"Perfect."

While Robert went off, David tracked down Cait, who had just finished bandaging someone's wounded arm. "Hey," she said, standing, "how are things proceeding?"

"Well. We're moving out soon. Will you do me a favor and canvas the upstairs area? I really didn't get a chance to actually look through it last time I was here."

"Sure."

"And *please* be careful on that catwalk. It's not super stable."

"I will."

She gave him a quick kiss, and then headed off, marching fleetly up the metallic stairs. While she went and did that, David walked over to the nearest crate, one of several on an old, collapsed wooden pallet, long since rotted by time. The crates had held up pretty well, though. Robert hit it with the prybar, getting the wedge in between the lid and the crate itself, and they spent a moment muscling it open. It came off with a pop and Robert reached into his pocket. He pulled out a lighter and lit it, helping them see the interior.

"Pants?" he murmured.

"Yeah..." David said. There were a bunch of pants inside. David pawed through them. They were heavy material, a bit baggy, gray, kind of stretchy. "All right, let's get another one open..."

They spent the next ten minutes prying open crates, as Cait returned from upstairs with, among a few other things, a crowbar, and Evelyn started helping them, given she was the strongest. They found more clothes, shirts and underwear and boots and socks, which *were* helpful. They also found a whole section of crates that were empty, for whatever reason. They were sealed, but empty. David wondered about that. Maybe they'd just been storing crates?

And then, finally, one whole section began revealing sections of chainlink.

"This is exactly what we needed," Cait muttered. "This is sturdy stuff, too. We could actually apply a whole second layer to our fence, not just repair the holes. There has to be ten crates of this stuff!" she said, sounding excited as she looked around.

"This is perfect," David agreed. "All right, grab whatever clothes you can, and anyone who can carry something heavier will help with the crates. We'll pair off, two people to a crate, and let's see how many we can get home in the first go."

"All right, people!" Robert called. "Pack it up! We're going to our new home!"

There was a cheer, and David felt a warm, happy sensation shoot through him. *This* was helping people. This is what mattered.

He started packing.

. . .

"Okay...did I miss anything?" David asked, looking between Evelyn, Cait, and Ashley.

"I think you covered everything," Evelyn replied. She smiled. "You're doing well, babe."

"Yeah, I'm impressed," Ashley said.

David ran through it all one more time. They'd managed to get the new group of survivors back to the campgrounds. It had been shaky there for a moment, as they'd had to fight off a pack of wildcats, but no one else had been injured, and they'd gotten home.

After sorting people out as best they could among the cabins, ultimately dividing them up between three cabins, he'd made sure the supplies that had been dropped off in the first floor of the main office was secure, and then had sent April out to check on everyone, given she was the medic among them. He'd then checked in with Amanda, made sure nothing had gone wrong in his absence, (and again promised to come see her tonight, she was rather insistent), and had gathered up the others.

He'd decided to have Ashley and Evelyn organize a party of people to go back to the warehouse and begin salvaging the supplies there.

Which left him with Cait and Jennifer.

"Okay, so where are *we* going?" he asked.

"We should tackle the bunker," Jennifer replied, and Cait nodded.

"Okay then, we'll do that. I can also swing by the hospital, I can see if they have any birth control," he said.

Ashley smirked suddenly. "Oh yeah...that's a thing now, huh? Yeah, you'd better, or you'll knock up Amanda."

"And Lena," Cait murmured.

"Lena?" he asked.

"You didn't see the way she was just *staring* at you?" Cait asked. "She *really* wants you, and she is *beautiful.*"

"She *is* very beautiful," he agreed. He looked at Evelyn and Ashley. "Be careful out there, okay?" he asked.

"We will. You be careful, too," Evelyn replied. He gave her a kiss, and when he went to do the same with Ashley, she grabbed him and kissed him hard.

"We need to hook up again, and soon," she said.

"He's gonna have to find the time," Cait murmured.

"Yeah, I'll, uh...I'll make that happen," he replied.

Ashley laughed. "Good. Come on, Evelyn, let's get this over with."

They headed out of the room. David took the time to make sure that his weapon was functional and loaded, and that the safety was on, that he had spare ammo, and that his pack was refilled with the appropriate supplies for going out into the dangerous world. Although this time he did pack a few more extra meds, just in case.

"Okay," he said, after Cait and Jennifer had done the same, "let's do this."

...

"Jennifer...I have a question," Cait said.

"Yeah?" Jennifer replied cautiously.

They had just crossed the bridge over the river once more, and were now plunging into the forest that was so heavily infested with stalkers.

"Now, please don't take this the wrong way, this is more curiosity than anything else. But...when we first met, you didn't even want to let us into your house, let alone work with us. But you've been spending days with us now. And again, I like you a lot, *obviously,* given what we did last night, but...what changed your mind?" she asked.

David had to admit, he was curious, too. She'd been reluctant to let them into her house when he, Cait, and Ellie had gone to ask for her help with the hospital's generator, even though there was a terrible snowstorm coming on. She *had* let them in with just a little pushing from Ellie, but still. The Jennifer he now saw was so...

Different.

She was still cautious and anxious, but she was so much more expressive and talkative and open. It was great to see.

"Well, honestly? It was David."

"Really?" he asked.

"Yeah. I don't know, that night we...you know, when you had sex with me, I mean, it was unreal. I took a while to process it. I felt like I was missing something, because for a long time, I just couldn't believe that it had happened as it appeared to have happened."

"What appeared to have happened?" Cait asked.

"That an attractive man, who wasn't a wraith and who didn't have some weird, overt fetish for wraiths, had not only had sex with me with no ulterior motives beyond wanting to have sex, but he actually *enjoyed* it. All of it. He enjoyed *me.* Someone I was attracted to had sex with me and it went great. That still feels so unlikely, so impossible, really. But that encounter was kind of like...a way back. Like, the first step on a path I had thought was lost to me. Because I've had some *bad* experiences with people.

"Human, rep, goliath, whatever. They've all hated me. It got to be so that I just gave up, I wanted to be alone. And sex is...it's intimate in a way that nothing else is. I'm not sure I would call it the *most* intimate thing, but it is unique in how it feels and what it is. I hadn't had it in a long time before I had it with you, David.

"And that just reminded me of what it was like to be *really* connected with someone. You didn't just give me the physical pleasure of sex, the release of an orgasm, you made me feel...human, again. If that makes any sense. You made me feel like a *person* again. Does that make sense?" she asked, looking at him and Cait.

"Yes, Jennifer, it does," David replied quietly.

"I'm sorry, am I being weird?"

"No, not at all," David replied. "I just...didn't realize it was, I guess, *that* serious for you. I mean, yes, you're right. I like you, I'm attracted to you, I wanted to make you feel good. To be clear: I'm *glad* that it helped you. I'm just surprised."

"Why?"

MISTY VIXEN

"I just..." he wasn't sure how to say it.

"I think he's having trouble with the concept that he helped you to the degree that he helped you," Cait said.

"Yeah, that sounds about right."

"Well, you did. I'm telling you right now. I mean, obviously it didn't just fix everything. But it reminded me, and then I got lucky, because I met Vanessa, and Katya, and the nice people at the hospital. They're all at the very least polite to me, some are actually warm. I'd call those two my friends, even. And then there's you, Cait, and Evie, and April, and Ashley. Everyone's been so...*nice* to me. And not in that weird, uncomfortable sort of way where people are just putting up with you. Everyone there, I mean, it's like...people don't even notice that I'm a wraith. Not, you know, your inner group," she explained.

"The fact that you're a wraith doesn't define who you are, not with us," Cait said firmly.

"And that is...*deeply* appreciated," Jennifer replied softly. "So, I mean, that's what's different. I'm around people that I actually like, and who actually like me, and it's reminding me how much I miss being around people."

David was considering asking the obvious follow-up question: how long do you think you'll want to stick around?

But then he heard a twig break somewhere nearby, and all three of them froze, aiming in different directions, as they'd all already drawn their pistols. David looked around, trying to contain the fear that was rising in him. Dead trees and skeletal bushes hugging the snowy ground surrounded them in all directions, broken up by the occasional path or clearing. For a few seconds, they were all silent, their breaths foaming on the air, the only sound that of the river somewhere behind them.

And then he caught movement. There, to his left, a figure slipped between the trees. And then another one. And then *another* one.

"Shit, I've got like four of them on my side," Cait whispered.

"Same," Jennifer muttered.

"Me too," David growled. "Fuck, get ready."

As soon as one of them showed themselves on his end, David fired off a shot. It was good, taking the thing right in its forehead and sending it flopping bonelessly to the snow. Another three hopped out from their hiding places and began sprinting furiously towards him, letting out awful shrieking noses.

David immediately began squeezing the trigger, tracking the first one and shooting it twice in the chest, putting it down, then shifting the barrel and taking another one in the shoulder. He missed twice, then got a great shot into its open, screaming mouth. Two more appeared as the final survivor of the initial wave closed in on him.

David turned one of its dark eyes into an explosion of blood and gore.

It dropped to the ground at his feet, and then he emptied his pistol putting down the remainders. He hastily reloaded the sidearm as *another* two of the fuckers appeared. Behind him, he could hear Cait and Jennifer firing off their own shots.

No doubt this was drawing in even *more* attention. He ended up throwing another seven bullets their way, the first getting lucky and going into the head of the first beast, but the second damned stalker was a fast, nimble bastard, and it almost was upon him before he finally murdered it.

No more appeared, and behind him, Cait and Jennifer stopped shooting.

"Okay, let's go," he said.

They hurried on, not bothering to search the stalkers because they had no clothes, as they were transformed from the nymphs. David hardly knew anything about the nymphs, beyond the fact that they were inhumans who had taken to living in the woods and were somehow very attuned to nature.

They went naked and lived among the trees, typically. They were to land what the squids were to water, at least as far as he could tell. He'd never met either species personally, and had only ever seen a handful of them his entire life.

He'd seen a female nymph once, from far off, and…

Wow, had she been *very* attractive.

But there was something else that was nagging him. Why were there *so* many fucking stalkers? They seemed to own this part of the region, but he'd seen more than usual in other areas, too. There shouldn't be *this* many, *especially* after that mass murder Lima Company had carried out a few weeks ago. There had been like two hundred of the fuckers there. Maybe that was something they were going to have to deal with at some point.

About five minutes later, having to put down a few zombies and pause to perform quick searches of them, David, Cait, and Jennifer finally arrived at the bunker. It was still there, and there was still a goddamned *field* of unmoving lumps beneath the snow.

"Oh my God," Jennifer whispered, looking at them all. "Were these...are those *all* stalkers?"

"Yep," Cait replied.

"Holy fucking shit, *how* did you three survive that again?" she marveled.

"Lima Company had about a dozen full on assault rifles, distance, training, and luck. Plus we put down an appreciable number," David replied.

"Fuck."

"Yeah. I was pretty sure we were going to die," Cait murmured.

"Then let's hurry up," Jennifer said, and they started heading towards it. They got over to the bunker, which was just a squat structure, little larger than a shed, sitting in the middle of a huge clearing. David helped them make sure the area was secure, then decided it was time to make his pilgrimage to the hospital.

"I'm going to go check on the doctors," he said.

Cait smirked. "And get your birth control?"

"Yes, that too," he replied.

"Mmm...it's too bad," she murmured.

"What's too bad?" he asked.

"Call me a freak but I'm actually really turned on at the thought of you knocking up another woman." He stared at her. "What?! It's hot. I mean, it was *so* hot when we first fucked and that came out, right?"

"Yeah..."

"So yeah, it's really hot. I don't know why. But there's obviously *huge* ramifications to it. It's not something you do lightly." She shrugged. "Maybe we'll find another chick looking to get pregnant? God, that'd be awesome."

"You are *way* too awesome of a girlfriend," he said.

"Yeah, I mean, I gotta admit, I don't know anyone else who would not only be okay with their boyfriend impregnating another woman, but be actively *seeking* it," Jennifer said.

"What can I say? I'm a freak of nature."

"Yes, you are," he murmured, stepping up to her. He glanced around as he settled his hands on her hips. "Maybe–"

"No, we're not having sex in a frozen field of corpses," Cait said, laughing. "I am not *that* much of a freak."

"Fair point," he said. He kissed her. "I love you."

"I love you, too."

He gave Jennifer a good, long kiss on her cold lips and a firm hug, too. "I like you a *lot,*" he said to her.

She smiled and looked away briefly. "I like you a lot, too," she said softly.

"Now, as for planning, how long do you think you'll be out here?" he asked.

"I don't know. Not long, I don't think. I just need to study the lock for a bit, and also check the bunker over, see if there's anything I'm missing, maybe a secondary entrance or something," Jennifer replied.

"Okay. How about, when you're done, you head to the hospital? Either I'll make it back here before you're done, you'll make it there before I'm done, or we'll run into each other, since we all know which path to take," he suggested.

"Sounds perfect, love," Cait said.

"Okay. Good luck."

"You, too."

David began to leave the clearing.

CHAPTER FIVE

He only had to kill three stalkers on the way to the hospital.

It was three too many, because he was getting to hate them, but David felt like he got off pretty easy. And he reassured himself that Jennifer and Cait knew what they were doing. They were both fast and strong fighters, especially Cait.

For some reason, it was a bit easier to calm himself this time around, but as he came on final approach to the hospital, David suddenly realized why: he was thinking about sex. Specifically, he was thinking about sex with Vanessa, also with Amanda. He *had* to see her tonight, to see if this was what he thought it was, because good fucking *lord* did he ever want to bang the shit out of that married pussy.

But he needed birth control first, or at least some protection.

He hadn't seen either in a while.

As he approached the front door, he caught movement in the window overhead, and saw a familiar face looking down at him.

"Katya," he said.

"Hello, David. I was hoping to see you again," she replied with a smile.

"How's Vanessa?"

"She's fine, though she's a bitch to keep on bed rest." She paused and looked back. "Yeah, I fucking know you can hear me, hush it."

"Can I come in? I need a favor," David replied.

"Yeah, hold on."

She shut the window and he walked up to the front door. A moment later, it opened up, and then she was standing before him, looking him up and down. He found himself doing the same thing. Katya was the kind of woman who was intimidating and attractive all at once. She was a little like a more hardcore, brutal version of Lara in a way.

She had short brown hair, tanned skin, a pretty good build, (she was actually about as tall as he was), and a wicked scar down one side of her face. She was wearing a camouflage outfit similar to what Lima Company wore and had a pistol on her hip. She looked marvelously, dangerously attractive.

"So what's up?" she asked.

"Well, we're figuring things out over at our encampment now that the assholes are dead. I specifically came here because I wanted to know if you had any birth control I could start taking," David replied.

"Birth control?...*oh*. Because Cait's...yeah, okay. And you don't want to knock anyone else up," she said.

"You know?"

"Yeah. I mean, she came here to get checked out and get it confirmed."

"Oh, right. Duh."

"You know, I think you might be in luck. Why don't you go upstairs to mine and Vanessa's room, you know, the one where you banged the shit out of her last time, and I'll see what I can track down while you say hello to Vanessa. She's in her bed," she suggested.

"Okay. Thank you."

"You're welcome."

He headed off through the building, nodding to a few of the others as he passed them, as they seemed busy with their own tasks, and he moved upstairs to the bedroom he had indeed fucked Vanessa in not all that long ago. He found her laying in her bed with a stack of books. She'd taken a few gunshot wounds during the assault and he'd been worried about her.

"Hey, cutie," she said, grinning at him.

"Hi, Vanessa. Are you doing okay?" he replied, coming and standing beside her bed.

"Yeah, I'm fine. Although shit, I'm getting old," she complained. "That shit really took it outta me. I used to be able to take a few gunshots. Although maybe it's just because it's winter. I almost never fight in the winter and I fucking hate winter...what's up with you?"

"The usual: running all over the place, killing zombies, tracking shit down," he replied.

"Pounding pussy?" she asked with a smirk.

He chuckled and rubbed the back of his neck. "Yeah."

"Congrat–" She froze. "Uh...how's Cait?" she asked.

He laughed. "Don't worry, she told me. I know she's pregnant with my child."

"So it *is* yours then? She was in a bit of a daze when I heard about it."

"Yeah. I'm the only human guy she's been with for a while now. It has to be mine. And so we're going to become parents," David replied.

"Then congratulations. I'm very happy for you. Also, Katya's going to ask for your help, but first she's going to jump you," Vanessa said.

"I...really?" he asked.

"Yes. She's pretty pissed that I got to jump you last time. She's sexually frustrated."

"Really? Why?"

"Oh come on, David, you know why. Or shit,

maybe you don't, you fucked me pretty much without hesitation. She scares men. Not *all* men, obviously, but she's a little picky, actually. So it's hard for her to both find a guy willing to fuck her, and *also* that she's willing to fuck. And can you blame her? A lot of guys confident enough to screw her are cocky douches. But you're something special. You're brave, you're cute, you're respectful. I assume that's why you've got that little harem you've got," she said.

"I...wouldn't call it that," he murmured.

"Are you blushing? Call it whatever you will, but you've got like six women who want to do sex things with you on a regular basis. That's a harem."

He thought about it, and realized she was close to right. There were obviously Evie, Cait, and April, but Jennifer was becoming a regular, as was Ashley. And there *had* been Ellie. He frowned as he realized he'd have to update them on that.

"What's wrong?" Vanessa asked.

He heard footsteps coming up the stairs and Katya appeared. "You're in luck."

"Thank you very much," David said, accepting a small vial of pills.

"What's that?"

"Birth control."

"Oh yeah, that makes sense. But what's wrong?" she asked.

"Is something wrong?" Katya asked.

He sighed. "Ellie's gone."

Vanessa sat straight up. "*What?*" she demanded.

"Not dead!" he clarified, raising his hands. "She's not dead, at least as far as I know. No, she ran out on us. When Cait announced her pregnancy, Ellie flipped out, grabbed her shit, jumped out a window, and ran off into the forest in the middle of the night."

"Holy fucking shit, really?" Katya asked.

"Yeah. I don't really know *why* she freaked out, but there's probably a decent chance that she just...left. The whole region. And won't come back."

"Fuck," Vanessa muttered.

"That really sucks," Katya said, crossing her arms and frowning. "Does Cait know why?"

"She says she thinks she does, but it's Ellie's business, so..." he shrugged.

"Damn." She shook her head. "Well, if she's gone then she's gone, and we won't be able to find her, let alone make her come back. Um...that birth control works pretty simply. We managed to get our hands on a load of it, among other things, when we were coming into the region. It'll keep for a while longer. Basically, you just take one pill a month. Roughly every thirty days. That'll cover you and you won't knock up any more ladies."

"Really? It's that easy?" he replied.

"Yep. Kills your sperm. Tried, tested, and true. You *do* have to wait twenty four hours for it to kick in, though," she explained.

"Huh." He popped the top, rattled one out into his hand, and immediately dry swallowed it.

Both women laughed. "Got a hot date?"

"Uh...maybe," he replied. "It depends on how a meeting goes."

"I see. Well, for now, I've got two things to say to you. The first is that I'd like your company while I go do something. I found a watchtower that I want to check out. The second thing is that I want *my* turn with your dick," she said.

Vanessa laughed softly. Well, she had certainly been right.

"Both of those sound good, although..." He held

up the birth control.

"Oh. Right. Don't worry, I'm infertile. Had the test and everything a while ago. So we don't have to worry about that."

"Okay, perfect. The only thing is: I'm actually working on something with two of my people right now and they're going to meet me here. Would you be willing to either wait until they're here, or go with me to them? Then I'll go with you," he asked.

"Sure. Now take your clothes off, I want to be on top," she replied.

"Okay." He immediately began to undress.

She smirked. "Good." She started getting out of her uniform, kicking off her boots. "Also, when I say 'on top', that means that at one point I'll want to be on top of your face, riding your tongue. You good with that? Don't worry, I washed very recently."

"Fine by me," he replied.

"I knew there was a reason I liked you," she said, and got her sports bra off.

She had some wonderful tits. Firm, c-cups, topped with some beautiful, dark pink nipples. And she had abs. And even a few tattoos under her shirt. Holy fuck! She was *wicked* hot. She pulled down her pants and panties, revealing that not only had she washed recently, but she'd shaved, too. Her pussy looked smooth and beautiful.

As soon as they were both naked, Katya walked right up to him and kissed him on the mouth while wrapping him in a hug and pulling him against her. It was almost an aggressive kiss. Well, that made enough sense, given what he knew about her. He kissed her back, running his hands across her fantastically fit body, eventually settling on the swell of her ass. She had a fit and pleasantly sized ass, he found as he groped it.

Katya suddenly turned, bringing him with her as she did, walked him back a few steps, then pushed him onto her bed.

"Someone's horny," he muttered as he climbed backwards onto the bed, staring at her intently.

"Fuck yes, I am," she agreed, never breaking eye contact as she stalked towards him, then began crawling onto the bed until she was hanging over him, staring directly down at him.

Her scar seemed more obvious than ever, and more had been revealed as she had disrobed. She resumed kissing him, holding herself over him for a bit before laying her nude body against his own. She wasn't just warm, she felt hot to the touch.

They kept making out for several more minutes, and David lost himself in her, in this beautiful badass woman named Katya who wanted him, wanted him to touch her and kiss her and be inside of her, to pleasure her. It was as exhilarating and thrilling as ever when he hooked up with a new woman. Cait would probably be frustrated that she missed her chance to watch.

Oh well, he supposed he'd just have to screw Katya a second time while she was around. And she'd probably get horny enough watching to demand a round two threesome.

God, that would be amazing.

"Okay, handsome," Katya said, pushing herself up and getting onto her knees, looking down at him with that sure smile, "time for you to show me what that tongue can do."

"I'm ready," he replied.

"Good." She moved forward until she was straddling his face, settling into place over him, her knees on either side of his head. She rested her hands on the headboard. Her pussy was right over his mouth. He opened it and stuck his tongue out, sought her clit, and then knew he'd found it when her whole body shuddered and she let out a moan.

David got to work pleasing her.

As he listened to her begin to groan in ecstasy and licked at her clit over and over again, David began to wonder about the nature of control, sexual control specifically. Although it was something he was still investigating and experimenting with, he'd found that in general he looked to be the one with control. He also liked doing a bit of domination.

On the other hand, while he was okay and actually pretty turned on by women like Katya and what was happening right now, he didn't think he could ever enjoy passing over into the submissive territory. He didn't have anything against it, it just didn't work for him. Which was strange in its own way, considering how downright attracted he was to tough, badass women like Katya and Vanessa and Ellie and Cait.

And he actually liked the way Katya was riding his face right now.

Listening to her moan and cry out, looking up at her as she towered over him, feeling her run her fingers through his hair as he ate her out, it was a thrilling experience.

"Yeah, David! *Yes!* Fuck!" she cried.

"Would you do that for me?" Vanessa asked from where she laid on her bed, watching their sexual display.

He tried to respond, couldn't, and instead gave her a thumbs-up.

"Ha ha, awesome! I can see why Cait likes you

so much," she said.

"Yeah, me *too!*" Katya cried. "Ah!" She twisted and arched her back as he licked away at her clit, and suddenly pushed herself up. "Okay, time for sex," she said, shifting quickly down his body until she was over his cock, and then she was lining them up, staring down at him with wide, excited eyes, looking like a fearsome, battle-scarred warrior out of mythology.

She grinned savagely as she took his cock into her and then the pleasure hammered into him as she slid smoothly down his rigid length. He groaned loudly, reaching out and grabbing her hips.

"Oh fuck, Katya..." he groaned.

"That's right, David," she muttered as she began to ride him, putting her powerful hips to use, "that's right, just lay there and get fucked. Just fucking lay there and let me fuck you," she groaned, reaching out and gripping his shoulders tightly. She felt so fucking incredible inside, and for a moment he forgot about everything else. He forgot about his new responsibilities, his anxieties of running a colony and being a father, Ellie's abandonment, the ever-encroaching threat the undead hordes, and he just got fucked by this hot, fit brunette as another exceedingly sexy, nearly eight foot tall woman watched.

He knew he had to fix this problem of reproduction because he wasn't sure he was ever going to be able to go to using protection. Unprotected just felt...*way* too good. It would never be a problem with the inhumans, but obviously he and Cait were going to keep having sex after her pregnancy, and there were other women who he probably wanted to screw who were capable of getting pregnant. He groaned as Katya shifted positions and started going faster. Goddamn, she was *so* fit! And clearly very skilled at sex.

There was no hesitation, no fear, no awkward shifting on her part. She knew exactly what she was doing.

"Here, hold still," she murmured, then she began moving, and quickly got around so that she was facing the other way, showing him her really nice fucking ass. It was fit, but it also had some awesome padding to it.

David reached out and grabbed it as she began to ride him again, taking him into her hot, wet pussy again and again, shoving him deep in there and pleasuring them both.

"You are *so* fucking hot," he groaned.

"Oh yeah-*ah!*" she cried as he grabbed her hips and thrust up into her.

"Yes!" he cried and started fucking pounding her, pulling her hard against him, and he listened to her yell in surprised rapture.

"Holy shit this is really hot," Vanessa said.

"Keep...ah...going...gonna..." she trailed off as he kept screwing her and within a few more seconds, she suddenly let out a crying moan of pleasure as she started to orgasm.

"Ohhhhh *yes...*" David moaned loudly as he felt her pussy begin to flutter and spasm around his rock-hard cock.

He kept screwing her, going harder and faster, really drilling her pussy, and then he was coming inside of her, shooting his load into her sweet vagina. Both of them moaned and climaxed together, naked and sweaty and writhing in pleasure. It rose and rose and reached a crescendo within them, a blasting heat of total ecstasy, and then it fell, and they were left panting and sweaty before it, neither moving for a few moments.

After a bit, Katya got off of him and moved over to a washbasin to clean herself up.

"That was good," she said in a rather matter-of-fact kind of way, like she was evaluating something with a somewhat clinical detachment.

He laughed. "Is that all you have to say?"

"High praised, coming from Katya," Vanessa said.

"It often isn't good," Katya agreed. She finished cleaning herself up and abruptly dried, then began to dress. "You should get ready."

"Okay," he said, admittedly a little surprised by her change.

"David," Vanessa said as he got up. He glanced at her. "She gets like this after sex. Right after she comes. Don't let it bother you."

"Yes," Katya said as she began lacing up her boots. "I'm sorry, should have said something. When I get my horniness out of me, it kind of brings everything into clarity, and I get really motivated to do shit. You could say I become cold and focused, which wouldn't be wrong. Don't let my demeanor make you feel bad, to be clear," she looked up at him, "that was very good and I enjoyed it, and I want to do it again. But right now I want to do my job."

"Okay, I can appreciate that," he replied as he began washing himself up.

He actually kind of got it, but it was still surprising. Normally the women he hooked up with tended to get lazy and sleepy after he screwed them, and it was really a coin-toss for him. Sometimes he did too, often actually, but sometimes, like this morning, he came out of it raring to get to work.

Katya finished dressing and left the room, telling him she'd be waiting for him downstairs, and he looked at Vanessa as he pulled his clothes back on.

"So you're really okay?" he asked.

She smiled. "You're sweet. Yeah, I'm fine, David. I've been shot and stabbed before, in case you somehow missed the scars when we fucked. Goliaths are pretty hardy." He thought about Evie, and her gunshot wound, and how quickly she'd recovered.

"Yeah, that seems true." He lingered, wanting to talk with her more, catch up a bit. She'd been instrumental in helping them take out the thieves.

"You shouldn't keep her waiting. Don't worry, we can...catch up later," Vanessa said with a smirk.

"Okay." He hesitated. "Can I have a kiss?"

"Of course. Come here."

He came over to her and kissed her and, because he couldn't help himself, groped one of her enormous breasts. She laughed softly as he did, letting him linger in his kissing and groping, and then finally gave him a gentle push. "I know, I miss you, too. But Katya is not a patient woman."

"Yeah, I figured," he said. "See you later, Vanessa."

"Later, David."

He left the room and as he headed back downstairs, heard conversation and familiar voices. Sure enough, he found Katya talking with Cait and Jennifer. As he came into the room, Cait gave him a knowing smile.

"So, sounds like *someone* had fun without me," she said.

He grinned bashfully. "Yeah..."

"Next time, I want in," she said, looking at him, then at Katya.

"Fine by me, you're hot as hell," Katya replied. "Now, can we go?"

"Yes," Cait said. She looked at David as he finished walking over. "She's updated us on the situation. We're going to walk Jennifer most of the way to her house, then we three will continue on to the watchtower. Sound good?"

"Yeah, that sounds good," David replied.

"Okay, let's go," Katya said, and headed for the door.

They followed in her wake.

. . .

The walk through the woods was mostly uneventful. Mainly, he and Jennifer walked beside each other while listening to Cait and Katya catch up as they led the way. He and Jennifer held hands until they had to part ways when they got as close to her house as they were going to get on their way to the watchtower.

"I'll check out my tool and then I'll go back to the hospital when I'm done and wait for you there if I get done before you get back to my house, okay?" she asked.

"All right," David replied. He and Cait both gave her long kisses and hugs, and he was glad to feel the emotional warmth from her, the connection with her, not just between each other, but between her and Cait.

Jennifer seemed to have taken to both of them very, very well, and after all she must have been through, he was happy that she seemed to be taking so much happiness from their friendship. He watched her go, and then Katya urged them onward once again. He had to admit, Katya was impressive.

Most of the women he'd run into were, in their own ways, driven and determined, but he'd never actually seen Katya in action before, and she was a bit of a taskmaster. She chatted, but made sure to maintain a strict and sure pace, walking ever onward towards her next destination, seemingly hating to linger anywhere for too long.

And, as such, they managed to reach the watchtower in question within another ten minutes or so of following an overgrown but serviceable path through the woods. David kept an eye out for stalkers, as he figured they were at least skirting the edge of their territory. It was hard to tell where they were going to be.

The watchtower looked to be in pretty good condition, and it sat right near the northern edge of the forest, rising above the trees and probably giving a fantastic and commanding view of the area. David found himself wanting to be up there because honestly, sometimes, a good view was its own reward.

Especially if it was of a place heavy with nature, and even more so during winter. He hated winter, hated the snow, the cold, the ice, the winds that seemed like they just sliced right through you, but he couldn't deny that a winter landscape looked absolutely fucking beautiful in most cases. It was probably the only good thing.

They got to the base of the watchtower and began ascending it.

"How'd you find this place?" Cait asked.

"I was just out scouting, looking for cool new shit, supplies, killing undead wherever I found them. I'm trying to establish an area of safety around the hospital," Katya replied.

"Does it actually work?" David asked.

"I don't know. It's hard to tell. I mean, we're not dead yet, so..." She shrugged.

They reached the top of the watchtower and began to investigate it. It was basically a copy of the very tower he'd investigated not all that long ago for medical supplies. He wondered if Ellie had ever come here. As they entered the central room, it became obvious that the place had been lived in, abandoned, tossed, lived in again, tossed again, fought in at some point, and probably a lot of other things.

It had sat here for decades at this point. Hell, everything had. Most of the windows were broken out and shards of glass littered the floor, crunching underfoot. They set to work, investigating what there was left to be investigated.

They upended knocked over furniture, sorted through the drawers of a corroded metal desk that was still roughly intact, and picked through the refuse that littered the wooden floor. Cait found a few unlabeled cans hidden under a ripped open mattress, Katya found a knife and a few magazines of ammo stashed away in one of the drawers, and in one corner, beneath a broken chair, David managed to unearth an old paperback.

He looked it over for a moment, finding it to be in surprisingly good condition. It was some kind of science fiction book, what looked like a mixture of adventure and romance between a human and an alien.

How appropriate, given his own current situation, and who he was giving this to.

"You find another one?" Cait asked, looking over his shoulder.

"Yeah," David replied.

"You know, she's not the only one who loves books," she said.

He looked at her for a moment, then down at the book, then held it out to her. She laughed and accepted it. "Do you think she'd mind if I got it first?"

"I hope not," he replied. "Would she?"

"I was just teasing, David," Cait said, slipping the book into her pack. "I actually talked to her about this. I asked if she would mind terribly if, well, this exact thing happened, and you gave me some of the books you found. She said she would be happy with that."

"Okay good," he murmured.

"You think your other girlfriend would be upset if you gave Cait a book?" Katya asked uncertainly.

"It's not really that, it's...what it might represent," David replied. "I started getting books for April when we first met, and it was under rather...dire circumstances. She was hurt and miserable when we found her, and that isn't even going into how...anxious, she is. I wanted to make her feel better. So me bringing her books kind of became a thing. And I guess I was worried she might view it as *our* thing."

"Oh, okay. Yeah, I can get that. Something special," Katya replied.

"Yes, but don't worry, honestly she's thrilled with the idea of more people reading books that she's read so that we can talk about them," Cait said. She looked past him suddenly. "What's that?" she murmured, and began to walk around him.

He and Katya joined her, moving to the far window, showing the northern area beyond the forest's edge. There was an open field with several collections of trees and a frozen creek running through it.

It also had three buildings. They were curious buildings, kind of like sheds, kind of like cabins, except they clearly weren't. They were squat, rectangular structures with faded blue siding. "What *are* those?" he murmured.

"Trailers," Katya said.

"Trailers? Which are?" he asked.

"They have a few different uses. These are basically small structures people used to put on job sites. Like construction sites or tree-cutting operations. Basically they're really simple buildings you can set down easily and put offices or dormitories in. Kind of like a cheap and easy temporary home for workers," she explained.

"Oh, nice. You think there's anything cool in them?" he asked.

"Maybe. Worth checking out at least? You up for extending this trip?"

"Yes," Cait said, looking at David. He nodded.

"Okay then, let's go."

They made their way back down the stairs and took a moment to put bullets through the heads of a few zombies that had shown up to investigate their presence. They patted them down, but didn't find anything worthwhile among them, and then started making their way towards the trio of trailers situated in the clearing.

"You doing okay?" David asked. Cait seemed to have gotten quiet and a little unhappy since leaving the watchtower.

"I'm...okay," she replied. He looked at her, waiting. She sighed. "Okay, I'm a little...guilty."

"Why?" he asked. Then he glanced suddenly at

Katya. "Unless you want to discuss this later?"

"No, I don't mind," she murmured. "Katya's heard worse from me." Katya snorted, but otherwise kept silent. "I already talked about this with Evie, but...I feel bad. I feel like I just barged my way into your's and Evie's and April's relationship. I mean, I didn't even intend to, not at first. I liked you when we first met, and I definitely wanted to keep fucking around with you, but I never really knew it would go *this* far. I was already feeling uncomfortable with it, and then I got *pregnant* with *your* child. And that's just..." she sighed and trailed off.

"Did Evie tell you how she felt about that?" he asked.

"Yeah. And she's right. I'm trying to remind myself of that. You and I are the ones who *made* this child," she said, laying a hand across her belly, over her leather jacket. "But there's no reason the kid can't have more than two parents. I think Evie and April will make great parents, honestly. I just don't want them to resent me, you know?"

"They won't," David said. "You have to trust them."

"I do," she said. "I just...have insecurities."

"Don't we all?" Katya murmured.

"What are *your* insecurities?" Cait asked.

She laughed. "I'm not telling you."

"Oh, come on."

"Nope."

Cait sighed. "You're no fun."

That was about the time one of the doors to the trailers opened up and a woman holding a pistol stepped out. She aimed it at them. "That's close enough," she said, her voice low.

CHAPTER SIX

All three of them had reacted already, each drawing their weapons and aiming them back. "We're not here to cause problems," David said after a few tense seconds of silence passed.

"Then you should leave," the woman replied.

"You should piss off," Katya snapped.

"Katya!" Cait whispered harshly. She growled but held her peace.

"If that's really what you want, we'll go," David said, lowering his weapon. "But we can offer you help if you want it."

A look passed across the woman's face, a look that might have been desperation, and he was suddenly reminded of his first encounter with Jim at the gas station. He supposed it would be something he'd be running into frequently out here. It was something he *had* run into more than once wandering the wild, dozens of times actually, usually he either left or offered to trade, and sometimes the people were even open to it.

The woman eyed them suspiciously. David looked back at her neutrally. She looked tired, her skin pale, her dark brown hair a mess, clothes torn and stained in several places.

Finally, she slowly lowered the pistol she was holding.

"What kind of help?" she asked reluctantly.

"Well, at the very least, we could institute some kind of trade. We also have access to doctors who would be willing to help you if anyone is sick or injured," David said. He heard Katya grunt behind him and he looked back at her. "That *is* your credo, right? Help the helpless? Free to all?" he asked.

She sighed. "That's *their* credo, so yes. Within reason," she replied begrudgingly. David suddenly got the impression that Katya had severe trust issues with anyone she wasn't already familiar with. He didn't blame her.

He looked at Cait. "Should we offer to let them stay?"

"Probably," she replied. "But maybe we should get them to the doctor's first, if that's what they want."

"Hold on. Don't move," the woman said, then disappeared back into the trailer, not quite closing the door.

They waited a few minutes. David suddenly caught sight of movement in the window of another trailer and realized there were more people there. No doubt guns were trained on them. He tensed a little, but this didn't have the feel of an ambush. People usually either just sprung out, or they tried to entice you into coming closer, usually with attractive women or something. This felt more like as it appeared: a small, scared group of people.

A moment later, she reappeared. "All right, we do have people who should be seen by a medic," she admitted, sounding reluctant. "Are there terms?"

David looked at Katya, who sighed and stepped forward. "No, they'll see you for free. *However,* if you have something you could donate: food, ammunition, anything of trade value really, it would certainly be *appreciated,*" she emphasized.

"Fine," the woman said. "But all of us are going...and we're taking all our belongings with us."

"All right," David said. The barely sub-textual message being: *so don't bother trying to rob the buildings while we're gone.*

"What a fine day this turned out to be," Katya muttered.

"We'll swing back by and search them later," David replied. "Then we'll pick up Jennifer while you take them back to the hospital. Sound good?"

"Fine," Katya replied.

They watched as the woman disappeared back into the trailer for another few minutes, then came out and walked over to the second trailer, where she opened the door and stepped inside. Not long after that, several people began to come out. David counted nine in total, four of them children of varying age. One of the group was an old man, the rest appeared to be somewhere between his own age and middle-aged. He wondered what their story was, what had brought and kept them together. A few of them did indeed look sick, and they all looked miserable: tired, pale, some of them shivering, most of them scrawny.

Fuck, they had to help them.

"Come along," David said.

They began to make their way back through the forest.

...

It felt weird, coming back to Jennifer's place, but in a good way.

When they'd reached that fork in the road, he and Cait had split off after confirming that Katya was indeed okay with leading them back to the hospital. After seeing the kids and the generally poor condition of the group, her expression had softened a lot, and she seemed a little less grim. Which was good to know.

Empathy was an important thing. It had been a simple process to walk back to Jennifer's place, he was glad to find, now that Ellie wasn't around to show them the way there again. He pushed that thought aside yet again.

Everything seemed to remind him of her.

They knocked on the door and a moment later, it opened up and revealed a smiling Jennifer. "Tell me you have good news," Cait said as they walked in.

"I do. Uh...sorta," she replied.

"Sort of?" David asked, closing the door behind them.

"Yes. So, the device that I have, it *will* break that specialized lock on the bunker. Also, there's no other way in, unless I missed something somewhere, though I don't think that I did. But the point is: we have a way in. The problem is that the device in question is broken, and I need two parts to repair it.

"The good news is that they aren't incredibly uncommon, the bad news is that they're just uncommon enough to be a bit of a pain in the ass to find. I've been thinking of places we might find them, looking over the maps I have of the region, and I've come up with two locations," she explained as she led them deeper into her house, then into the kitchen, where the counters were littered with papers and parts.

"Okay, where?" Cait asked.

"The first is the radio tower, built up on the mountain. The second is that factory on the far side of the lake, Ellie said you and her once tried to go there?"

Cait groaned loudly. "Yes. That fucking factory..."

"What's wrong with it?" David asked.

"It was *infested* with vipers. I mean just like crazy. Fucking *hundreds* of them."

"Great," he muttered. "You think it's still that bad?"

She sighed angrily. "I don't know, maybe. It's impossible to tell. It's been months since we've gone there. But honestly, with all the activity we've been seeing from them, it's really likely. Or maybe all the activity we've been seeing is because they've moved on to other places?"

"Well, considering our options, I guess we don't have a choice. Unless," he glanced at Jennifer, "is it possible that we might find both parts you're looking for at the radio tower?"

"It's...possible," she replied.

"But is it *likely?*" Cait asked.

She shook her head. "No, not likely. Definitely not likely."

"Fine. Then we go to the radio tower tomorrow," David said.

"Tomorrow? We could almost surely make it there and back today," Cait asked.

"We need to get those people back, and get them settled, and honestly, we really need to start making progress on repairing the fence. Now that we actually have the means, the longer it sits undone, the more uncomfortable I get," he replied.

She sighed. "Yeah, you're right."

"People?" Jennifer asked uncertainly.

"Yes, we found some people in dire circumstances out in the middle of nowhere. They're at the hospital right now, getting checked out. I figured we could offer them a place to stay," David replied. "Don't worry, Jennifer, we're not going to let anything happen to you."

"Yes, you can count on that," Cait said, stepping closer to her and putting a hand on her shoulder. "You can trust us."

"I know. I *do* trust you, I just...meeting new people always scares the shit out of me, because it's always a gamble. Will they tolerate me? Hate me? Try to kill me? Mock me? Most of the options are shitty," she muttered.

"I understand," Cait said.

"Do you?" she asked, looking at her with her dark eyes.

"No," Cait admitted, "not truly, not in the way you understand it. But I *appreciate* your situation. If you really want, you can stay here for the night, and we can come get you tomorrow."

"No, that'd be like an extra hour out of your way, since the radio tower is so much closer to your place. And besides, I don't really feel like being alone anymore. I thought I'd be happy coming here, back to my house, but honestly? I've just been eager for you two to come back. I'd really like to spend the night at your place again," she said.

"That's fine. You're always welcome," Cait said. She thought about it. "What if you and I went on ahead of David, and he dealt with the people and then led them back? You wouldn't even have to leave the main office until tomorrow."

"I don't want you going to extra trouble for me," she said unhappily.

"It's not extra trouble, Jennifer."

She looked back and forth between them for a moment, then nodded. "Thanks."

"You're welcome. Do you need anything else?"

"No," she said, putting the device into her pack and then pulling the backpack on. "I'm ready to go now."

"Okay, let's do it."

...

They made their way back towards the hospital and split off as they reached it.

David walked up to the front door and found Katya standing out front, smoking a hand-rolled cigarette, looking irritable.

"Hey, what's wrong?" David asked.

"Nothing," she muttered. "Where's Cait?"

"She went on ahead of me with Jennifer. How are they doing?" He came to stand next to her.

"They're fine, for the most part. One of the kids has a sprained ankle, two of them have colds, one has an infection that's going to take a week of meds to clear, and they're all malnourished," she replied. "But it's nothing serious. They can recover from everything if they get one good week of warmth, regular meals and sleep, and some meds."

"So what's wrong then? Obviously something's wrong," David said.

She took a long pull on her cigarette and blew out a cloud of smoke in an unhappy sigh. "I was just...reminded."

"Of what?"

"That I've seen a lot of shitty people do a lot of shitty things, and it corroded my trust almost to the breaking point, and it made me hate people in general. And I've spent years trying to recover from that, to come back from the brink of full misanthropy. And today just reminded me that it's still way, *way* too easy for me to just slide right back into distrust and hatred. A few years ago, I'd have called you weak and stupid for trusting those people, and if they took advantage of your trust, then I'd have said you deserved it."

"Wow," he murmured.

She sighed. "Yeah."

"What changed your mind? Or made you want to change?" he asked after a few moments of nothing but a coldly blowing wind passed.

"I met this group. They saved my ass. I'd gotten shot when the group I was with got raided. Got left behind in the panic, managed to slip away. I was hiding out somewhere, it was a gut shot, it got infected and I almost died. But they found me, and they healed me, just because they thought it was the right thing to do. Came across me at random. They asked for my help when they learned how skilled I was at combat and tracking, I wanted to say no, but honestly, it wasn't like I had a lot else going on, and something about them just...I don't know, called to me. Something was telling me that I should do this, and that something was right."

Neither of them spoke for a little while after that. Katya finished off her cigarette and flicked it into the snow, then stared out into the forest for a few moments, crossing her arms. David waited. He had the idea that she wanted to say something.

Finally, she said, "Thanks. What you're doing, and Cait, and Jennifer, and your people over at your home, it's important. It's the right thing to do. I've seen the other side of the coin. The side where everyone's out for themselves, and no one trusts each other, and everything is reduced down to cold calculation, trying to fuck the other person over faster and harder than they can fuck you over, because you automatically assume they're going to.

"That place, that headspace, it's one of the most toxic, corrosive things I've ever had to endure. And sometimes that's what it takes to survive. But what people like Donald and Vanessa and the others in there, people like you and Cait and Evie, have shown me is that sometimes it's better to trust and get burned, than to try and burn everyone who wanders into your line of sight. And sometimes I...start to forget that."

David wasn't sure what to say.

"Don't worry," she said, as if she could read his mind, "you don't have to say anything. I wouldn't know what to say either. I just wanted to thank you for helping, and listening."

"You're welcome," he said finally.

She laughed softly. "You're a good guy. Don't change."

"I'll try."

"Good. Come on."

They headed into the hospital, where several quiet voices were overlapping. David hung around in the main room as he saw Donald and the woman from before that he'd spoken with, presumably the leader, talking quietly. He waited. Katya walked deeper into the building, disappearing through one of the doors, probably to help, given her expertise.

The woman glanced at him, said a few quick words to Donald, who nodded and followed after Katya. The woman then walked over to him, looking almost...regretful.

"Hi," she said as she came to stand before him. "Uh, my name's Lindsay."

"David," he said.

"...sorry about earlier."

"It's fine," he replied. "Honestly, I get it. Times

are *very* stressful."

She heaved a long sigh. "Yes, they are. But this is a fucking godsend," she said, looking around at the hospital. "The people here are very nice, very helpful. So were you. Um...where's the other? The redhead?"

"Cait went on ahead of me back to our home. Which I was hoping to talk to you about. What are your plans for the immediate future?" he asked.

She laughed bitterly. "Don't die," she replied. "Which...I don't know. I mean, we were going to shack up in those trailers."

"Would you be amenable to living in a small community?"

"I guess it would depend. Where is it? How many people are there? How defensible is it? Who's in charge? What's expected of us? Are you going to fuck us over?"

"It's about a half hour's walk from here, farther to the south, over a river. Right now there's about...thirty people living there. We're set up inside of an old campground. It's got a fence that we're in the process of repairing right now, actually. We have someone on guard at all times, and the area we're in isn't highly active with undead. We recently eliminated a gang of assholes who burned down another settlement I was in."

"Eliminated as in..."

"As in we murdered every last one of them. This was after they mounted *several* assaults on us and others, including this building, threatening murder and rape."

"Oh...wow."

"As for who's in charge. Myself and the redhead, Cait, and another woman, Evelyn, are all officially in charge, though we are admittedly still setting everything up. This kind of just...happened. Evelyn and myself and another woman found this place and started living there, and then we ran into other people in desperate situations, survivors from the burned-down settlement, and offered to let them stay, and over the past month it's just kind of coalesced into a settlement.

"As for what's expected of you: pulling your fair weight. So, doing jobs like chopping firewood, guard duty, picking plants, hunting game, babysitting, pretty much whatever needs doing. And we're reasonable. Jobs and hours are negotiable, and you're free to leave whenever you want. And no, we aren't going to fuck you over," David said.

She sighed softly, staring at him for a long while. "It sounds too good to be true," she said finally, frowning.

"I know. Believe me, I understand. We ran into another group today in almost exactly the same situation you're in now. I had this exact conversation with them. Also, the only caveat I want to add is that, for the moment, it *will* be a tight fit. While we do have enough cabins, not all of them are in living condition, and we're working on fixing that. However, I *will* make sure that everyone is in at least livable conditions before the day is through. That I can promise. Again, it might be a tight fit, but I'm not letting anyone freeze or go hungry." He paused, considering. "Actually, there is *one* more caveat I need to mention."

She tensed. "What?"

"We are a mixed community. I know some people have problems with that. Everyone is welcome, and we don't tolerate racism. And we *do* have a wraith working with us. We also presently have a rep, some jags now," (he'd seen a few jags in Robert's group), "and a goliath–"

"A goliath?" she asked sharply.

"Yes...Evelyn. She's the other woman in charge." Lindsay frowned sharply and looked down. "What's wrong?"

"I...we ran into a goliath a few months ago. A man, he was...cruel. A tyrant. He ran a settlement. We stayed there a while, and then it got so we couldn't leave, he wouldn't let us. He killed several people, and..." she trailed off.

"I'm so sorry," David said. "But I can completely assure you that Evelyn is very, very kind and reasonable. She's a wonderful woman."

Lindsay slowly nodded. "Yes, I can't turn this down just because of a bad experience once with a goliath. Just...some of the children might be afraid."

"I understand."

She met his eyes again. "I'm going to speak with the others, but I'll say now that I'm almost certain we'll accept this deal. The doctors here have recommended bed rest for several days, so we'll need some time to recover..."

"Don't worry about that. First we'll get you settled, then you can heal and gain your strength back. And we're always approachable. If you have a concern or an idea or really anything to say, you can absolutely approach any of us and tell us."

"Okay, we'll keep that in mind...thank you." She hesitated further. "I really hate to ask but..."

"Yeah?"

"My daughter. She..." she sighed. "She left her stuffed animal back at the trailer. It's...it's a zebra. I intended to go back and get it, but this place seems so dangerous, and I'm so exhausted and weak because we haven't had any food for almost two days now, and not a lot of food before that..."

"I'll get it," David said. "I think Katya, the brunette woman with the scar, was looking to go back there anyway. That's why we were there in the first place: looking for supplies. We'll head back while everyone here finishes up with their examinations and treatments and rests a bit."

"Thank you so much," she said. "I really, truly appreciate it."

"You're welcome."

David went to go track down Katya.

...

The day played out about as he'd hoped it would after that.

He and Katya made their way back to the trailers, putting down a handful of zombies and stalkers that had the misfortune to cross Katya's path, and then spent an hour performing a thorough search of the three structures. One was almost totally empty, but the other two at least had some stuff in them.

They found some food, some ammo tucked away in a plastic bag behind a drawer in a desk, some office supplies, a little medical pack, and some nails and screws and bolts, and the zebra he was looking for. He gave everything save for the zebra to Katya, since it was her expedition, and he honestly considered the pussy she'd given him a fair enough compensation. She'd laughed when he'd told her as such and accepted.

Upon getting back to the hospital, he found everyone patched up, a little more rested, and ready to go. And he was particularly happy to reunite

Lindsay's daughter with her lost zebra. From there, he'd escorted the group back to the campgrounds, and luckily didn't run into any hostiles.

They all seemed pretty shaken, and he was eager to get them to a place of safety and security. There was little talk among them as they walked, but it picked up once they were actually inside of the campgrounds. David then got to work sorting them out.

He, Evelyn, Cait, and April took a little while to figure out which cabins were habitable, and ultimately they managed to squeeze most people into one of the three bedroom cabins after taping some canvas into place over a broken window, and getting Lena and Chloe to agree to share their cabin with Lindsay and her daughter.

Chloe seemed reluctant, but Lena made her say yes. David felt her pain. It would be difficult to do sexy things with people sharing your space, and he promised to get the other cabins fixed as soon as possible.

The priority, however, remained the outer fence. Evelyn, Ashley, and their team had managed to bring back all the rest of the crates holding the new fencing material, and a few other crates holding blankets and pillows, he was very happy to see.

They needed those now more than ever. Since he had a rough idea of what he was doing, he joined Cait, Ashley, Amanda, and several of the others in mending the rips, tears, and holes in the fence. They could set up a second layer after they got the bare minimum done, he figured.

That took up all the remaining daylight, the twilight, and some of the darkness. They managed to at least get the worst of the holes patched. Although there were still some weak spots, something would have to make noise to get in now. After that, they had dinner, and spent a little while talking about how they were going to proceed tomorrow.

They ultimately decided that he, Cait, and Jennifer would make the expedition to the radio tower, while Evie, Ashley, and April continued to oversee things at the encampment, including making a few more pilgrimages to the warehouse to finish clearing it out of any remaining supplies.

After dinner, David had gone to wash up, and had asked each of the three women in his life how they felt about him having sex with Amanda. Well, first with Katya, given he felt the need to update them on that. Cait obviously knew, Evie congratulated him, and April was impressed, given what she'd heard about the combat medic.

As for Amanda, Cait and Evie gave enthusiastic affirmations, and although she was down for it, April did warn him to ask her specifically if her husband had knowledge of anything happening and was okay with it.

He agreed with her there.

And that's what he was doing right now. Well, technically what he was doing right now was going over to Amanda's place to see what happened. It was still entirely possible that she had something completely unrelated to sex she wanted him to do or to talk to him about, although Cait said that he was definitely fucking some married pussy tonight.

Even if that was true, though, he still hadn't found any protection, and didn't know if she was fixed or not. Obviously she was fertile, she had a kid, but she might have somehow gotten surgery or maybe she'd found some birth control since then. He supposed he'd find out if it came up.

David walked across the cold darkness, happy to see that so many of the cabins were lit up, smoke coming out of over half a dozen chimneys. They had a real community now. At this point, it was a matter of getting settled.

And hoping nothing went wrong.

David knocked on Amanda's door.

The door opened and Amanda stood there before him, wearing a tattered white robe, looking marvelously sexy.

"Come in, David," she said with a confident smile, stepping out of his way.

He stepped inside and looked around their living area. There didn't seem to be anyone around. He looked back at Amanda Carlson. Her dark hair had grown since he'd last seen her, and she now wore it in a ponytail. Her skin was as pale as he remembered. At first he had mistaken her pallor for illness, but even now, though she looked much healthier and more put-together than their first meeting, she was still so pale.

It made her green eyes stand out in stark contrast. She looked a little less skinny, which was good, it meant she was getting regular meals. The robe was knotted tightly around her waist, and it clung nicely to her figure.

"So, David," she said, "come with me."

"Okay."

She led him across the living room and through one of the doors, into a bedroom, what had to be her and her husband's bedroom. Several candles burned, some on a dresser, some on the nightstands to either side of the bed, giving the place a pleasant atmosphere. Moonlight spilled in through the top of the curtain, which was firmly closed, covering almost the whole window. Amanda took a seat at the foot of the bed, and patted the spot next to her.

Her wedding ring glinted in the light.

David sat down next to her.

"So...what is this, exactly?" he asked.

"I suppose that's a fair question. In case you haven't picked up on it, I've been flirting with you," she said, and she laid her hand on his thigh. He felt a pulse of powerful lust hit him. "And, unless I'm off my mark, you've been responding quite well to it."

"Uh, yes...yes, I have," he replied.

"Good. I'm glad. Now, I've already spoken with Cait about this, and I talked briefly with Evelyn about it. April is...difficult to get hold of, I've noticed."

"She's very...private."

"I understand. She's got a lot of anxiety, I think. I was a lot like her when I was much younger. But anyway, what this is, specifically, is: I want to have sex with you. You're a very handsome young man, and it has been too long since I enjoyed the company of such a man." She began to move her hand up and down his leg. "Now, to be clear, my husband and I are in an open marriage, though it's been a bit closed up until just recently. More out of necessity than desire, we just didn't have the time to go fucking other people. But now he's caught the eye of a young jag woman from the new group you brought in, and...I've caught *your* eye."

"You definitely have," he said.

"I'm sensing some hesitation."

He chuckled. "You're sharp."

"Yes, I am," she agreed.

"I am fucking ecstatic to do this with you. Cait, Evie, and April all encouraged it. So no problems there. The only issue is...can you get pregnant?" he asked.

"Yes, I can. After learning of Cait's recent development, I talked to her about it, and she said you would try to seek some form of birth control..."

"I have, and I found it. I took some. The only problem is, it doesn't kick in until tomorrow night," David replied.

"Ah. Yes. Damn," she murmured, glancing briefly to the door. "Unfortunate, but not unsalvagable. Jim is with that jag woman right now, Ben is hanging out with a new friend of his, and my daughter has gone off for a sleepover at Ann's house. It was a little difficult to make all of it line up..." she said, thinking.

"Well, we can definitely do sex things in *my* place," he said. "My girlfriends *really* like to watch, if you're down for that."

"Hmm...I might be. But I have you tonight, for the next hour or so. I think that's as long as I'll risk it. Obviously, Ben doesn't know what's happening, and I'd rather he didn't. It's not like we're his parents, but it would be...awkward."

"I get it. So...you wanna do foreplay then?" he asked.

"Yes. I would love that," she said.

And he leaned in and kissed her, because he was so excited about what was about to happen that he couldn't hold himself back any longer. She responded in kind immediately, kissing him back, settling her hands on him, tilting her head and moaning. Oh wow, this was happening. This was really happening. He was making out with a married woman and...

He was...

Slipping his hand into her robe and hell yes, there was her breast, her bare breast, a nice and firm b-cup, fitting nicely into his hand. He groped her and the robe fell down her shoulder, revealing more of her pale, pale bare skin.

She was remarkably beautiful, something a little daunting about her, the contrast of her dark hair and wild green eyes against her pale as snow skin. She kept making out with him, breathing more heavily, her robe falling off her other shoulder, revealing her bare chest. He kept kissing her and then she pushed him down onto his back and mounted him easily. She stared down at him briefly, grinning, her eyes wide, and resumed kissing him.

She was such a good kisser.

And her lips. She had really nice fucking lips, really luscious lips that were so kissable.

They made out passionately in the flickering candlelight and he felt very strange about the whole thing as he ran his hands across her tight, fit body beneath the blankets. On the one hand, this was fucking awesome. He was making out and in a bed naked with a woman certainly over a decade older than he was, and she was sexy as hell, and clearly she was into him. But he couldn't ignore that ring on her finger, and that's what was giving him at least some pause, if only inside his own head. Although obviously he wasn't going to pause in actually doing this.

He wanted to do this. He wanted to fuck her. He wanted to stick his cock everywhere she'd let him and blow his load all over her face and down her throat and suck on her wonderful, firm, pale tits as much as she'd allow him to. There was no question there. It was the fact that she was married. He believed her about the open marriage, and he didn't think there was a problem with being in such a relationship, but still...

What was the problem? Everyone involved, and even those not involved directly, had all offered happy consent. So what was making him hesitate (mentally speaking, obviously, given the fact that he had pretty much dove into bed with her)?

Maybe it was because it wasn't just that he knew he was fucking around with another man's wife, it was that he *liked* it specifically *because* she was another man's wife. She wasn't cheating on her husband to be with him, but...at least at a glance that's what it resembled. There was a dark thrill to it, and he couldn't help but be at least a little paranoid that they were going to get walked in on and this whole thing was going to blow up.

And that was it: he didn't like that he *liked* the idea of fucking another man's cheating wife.

David fitted his hand in between her firm, slim thighs and his fingertip sought, and found, her clit. She moaned as he touched it, then began to massage it.

"Oh *yes...*" she moaned loudly. "That's just the perfect spot, David."

"Amanda..." he groaned, and resumed kissing her, rubbing her clit harder.

Was it so bad that the idea got him off? From what he gathered, everyone liked something fucked up. What you *liked* and what you *did* were two totally different things. And besides, how many people fantasized about fucked up things? Roleplayed in the bedroom? As long as they were both cool with it, what was wrong?

He slipped a finger inside of her and told himself to relax, he was overreacting to nothing. So what if he got off on cheating? It wasn't like he was *going* to.

God, could he even cheat? Was there anyone he could fuck that would piss off his girlfriends? Well yeah, if he fucked a woman who was cheating, they'd probably not be cool with that. Or maybe they would? Maybe they got off on it, too? Probably not April, but Cait? Evie? Maybe.

He was thinking way too much about this, but that's what happened when you were in the dim light of a woman's bedroom with her naked and pressed up against you, kissing you, doing sexy things with her.

Or, at least, that's what happened to *him*.

"Oh, David! I'm going-oh! I'm going to come, don't stop!" she begged.

He stepped it up, switching back to her clit, rubbing it vigorously, and she writhed and twisted and twitched against him, breaking the kiss and laying flat on her back, eyes squeezed shut, panting and moaning furiously, and then–

"*Oh!*" She was coming. He'd made her come. He kept rubbing her clit and she pressed a hand over her mouth, crying out in intense passion as the orgasm rolled through her. He kept her going, helped her ride the wave as it crested, and then she was coming back down, panting, eyes squeezed shut. After a moment, she opened them and smiled at him. "That was wonderful."

"Yes, it was," he agreed. "You look *so* wicked hot when you come."

"Thank you. Now...lay back and let me show you what my mouth can do."

"Yes, ma'am," he replied, immediately beginning to shift.

He ended up on his back and she got down between his legs, staring up at him as she ran her fingers up and down his cock. "So...this is the cock that pleasures a goliath, hmm?"

He laughed. "That's not the first time I've heard that."

"I bet."

"And two goliaths now, actually."

"Oh *really?* My my, you *do* get around," she murmured. "Tell me about your sexual escapades."

"Okay..." he said, then grunted as she licked across the head of his dick, sending sparks of ecstasy spiraling into him. He tried to focus as she kept licking. "Well, you know about Cait, and Evie, and April," he muttered.

"Mmm-hmm."

"We have a lot of sex. And I, um, oh wow that's good, I have sex with Ashley, too."

"She's a pretty little thing."

"Yeah, and she can fuck so good. And I've had sex with...ah! Yeah...one of the girls from Lima Company."

"Oh *really?*" she asked again. "I bet those military girls can *fuck.*"

"Yes. She was so very good in bed," he replied.

She laughed and then took his cock into her mouth, slowly sucking him off, putting her amazingly hot, wet, luscious lips to use.

"And I've had sex with another goliath, and today another human woman. She was definitely a real hardass and really, uh, rough in bed. And..." he hesitated. "And a jag woman, and a wraith."

She looked up at him, pausing briefly. "Anyone I know?"

"I'd...prefer not to say. I don't know how they'd feel about it. I mean, *I'm* thrilled to have fucked them, and I don't care who knows, but they might be uncomfortable with it."

"I respect that," she said, and resumed sucking his dick again.

"Oh my God, Amanda," he groaned, laying a hand over the back of her head. "You give really, really good head."

"Mmm-hmm," she agreed.

He laid back and let her work, watched her work, watched her amazing lips slip smoothly up and down his rigid shaft. Looked at her naked, slim, pale body. He thought about having sex with her. Having unprotected, amazing sex with her. About how she would look on her back, writhing in pleasure with her legs spread wide as she took his cock again and again as he pounded her fucking brains out.

Thought about how he'd be fucking another man's wife and–

"Oh *fuck!*" he moaned as his orgasm unexpectedly flared into being.

Amanda didn't miss a beat. She just kept sucking, just kept bobbing her head smoothly up and down, taking his load into her mouth, sucking it out, sucking him dry with a wonderful ease. He could hear himself moaning ecstatically as the pleasure blossomed and blasted through him. She sucked him dry, moaning as she did, and then his cock was dry kicking, nothing left to give, as she'd taken it all. He was finished, left panting and sweaty.

She grinned up at him after taking his cock from her mouth. "That was nice, huh?"

"Nice doesn't begin to describe it," he murmured.

"Well–" She froze as the front door opened. "Fuck," she snapped softly, getting up and snatching her robe.

"Amanda?" a familiar voice called uncertainly.

Ben, the young man they were essentially fostering at this point. Apparently he was back early.

"Just a minute!" she called. She looked at David. "Could you possibly leave through the window?" she asked softly, looking guilty.

"Yeah," he replied, quickly and quietly getting up and pulling his clothes back on.

"I'll be out in a minute," she called, pulling her robe on and knotting it tightly around her waist. She moved over to the dresser and took a drink from a bottle of water. David finished dressing quickly and moved over to the window. He pulled the curtains back and looked out. There was just another cabin directly across from him, and he couldn't see anyone around.

"Tomorrow night? Your place?" she asked as he opened the window.

"Yep," he replied.

"It was fun," she said.

"A lot of fun," he agreed, and slipped out.

As he headed out between the cabins, he heard the window close behind him, and then he looked out into the campgrounds. There was no one around, everyone inside at this point, and he wasn't too far from the main office.

Perfect. He tried not to look too suspicious as he made his way over to it, since it would be all too easy to get mistaken for an intruder by whoever was on watch. In fact, someone shined a light on him as he made for the front door and he froze.

"Who's that?" a familiar voice called. It was Robert, he realized, on top of one of the roofs with a flashlight and a rifle.

"Just me, just David," he called.

"Oh. Everything okay?"

"Everything's great. How about on your end?"

"I haven't seen shit," Robert replied. "Freezing, though."

"Sorry."

"Don't be, this is still a hell of a lot better than any of the shit I've put up with for the past several months. And my shift is almost over," he replied.

They said goodnight to each other then and David slipped into the main office. He heard people talking quietly upstairs and after making sure the ground floor was locked down and secure, he headed up there and found Evie, Cait, and Jennifer at the dinner table, going over several pieces of paper scattered about.

They all fell silent and looked up as he came in.

Cait grinned devilishly. "You look...a little shaken," she said.

He laughed nervously. "I guess I am. I had to sneak out the window," he replied.

"Oh?" Evie asked, straightening up. "Do tell."

He came over and sat down with them. "It was what you all told me it was. Although we didn't have sex, we didn't have protection and my pill hadn't kicked in yet, we did a lot of foreplay, made each other orgasm, so that was awesome. It's all on the level, don't worry about that, her husband's off with one of the newer people right now, actually. But Ben apparently decided to come home early and she doesn't want him knowing, figuring it'd just make everything awkward. So she asked me to sneak out the window and I agreed."

"Such a bad boy," Cait said, grinning even more broadly at him. "I take it you had fun."

"Oh yes. A lot of fun. And we're going to have sex here tomorrow. I don't know if she'll be okay with an audience or not." He yawned. "Fuck, I'm tired."

"You've had a long day. We all have," Evie said. "What's on the agenda for tomorrow?"

"Jennifer, Cait, and I are going to investigate the radio tower for parts she needs to repair her tool to crack open the bunker," David replied.

"That...might be dangerous," Evie murmured.

"I know, but...well, what isn't?"

She sighed. "That's a fair point. There's a few more things I want to get from the warehouse tomorrow, and then we'll be done with it. After that, I need to finish organizing all the new people. And April will want to tend to everyone. That's going to be a full time job for the next week or so, I imagine, given all the new people. And speaking of new people..."

"Yeah, I know, we're pretty much at capacity," David muttered.

"We need to find material to fix up the cabins," Evie said. "I thought there might be some in the warehouse, but there hasn't been, and I'm sure now there isn't going to be."

"After we find those parts, we can investigate the construction site, down in the valley," David replied. "Hopefully we'll find what we need there." He yawned again.

"Okay," Cait said, "time for sex and then bed." She stood.

"Yes," Jennifer agreed.

David got up, too.

"Go on, I'll be up in a bit. I need to finish these schedules," Evie said. "And don't wait for me to get started."

Cait took his hand and Jennifer's and began

leading them off. "I don't think I could even if I tried," she admitted.

CHAPTER SEVEN

To David's great relief, it looked like the weather was holding.

It had snowed a bit overnight, but that seemed to have stopped entirely. The skies were mostly clear overhead as they walked along the road, moving past the abandoned warehouse where Evie was going to come not long in the future with a small team.

He and Cait and Jennifer walked down the middle of the road, keeping an eye out for any hostiles, and they all seemed to be in high spirits. Even Jennifer, although he imagined it was hard to be in low spirits after having sex with three different people, all of whom worked hard to make you orgasm, which they all had managed to get at least a single orgasm out of her. She was exceptionally grateful for that.

"Do you have any idea what we might expect at the mountain?" Jennifer asked as they made their approach to it.

"No," Cait said after David shook his head. "No one I've known has really made much attempt to do this or come to this area. I don't know what we might run into. Maybe we'll get lucky and run into nothing at all."

David snorted. "When has that ever been true?"

She laughed. "Yeah, that's a fair point. Just wishful thinking on my part."

He could actually see the radio tower now. It was maybe halfway up the mountain, and he thought he could see a trail leading up towards it. He had mixed feelings about this whole thing. On the one hand, it would be good to check this place out, because it might actually have some cool shit up there.

This was a decently difficult to reach, out of the way place where someone might have gone out of their way to store stuff, then died or abandoned the area. Plus, there was sure to be a really cool view from up there.

On the other hand, it was probably going to be dangerous to get to. Between the trail which probably wasn't all that stable to begin with, and had surely degraded over the decades, and any hostile creatures that might be in the area, or even hostile humans. That was always a possibility. On the whole, he was going to be very glad when they were walking back home to the campgrounds, ideally with the parts in hand.

"I assume we're going to tackle the factory tomorrow, provided this doesn't give us what we want?" Jennifer asked.

"Yes," Cait replied.

"I think we're going to want at least a bit of help there."

"You think us, Evie, and Katya would be enough?" David asked.

"Probably," Cait said uncertainly. "The problem is, I have no idea what the conditions there will be like, but it makes sense to err on the side of caution..." She growled suddenly. "Goddamnit, Ellie. We could really use her help about now."

"Yeah..." Jennifer said sadly.

David felt her frustration, and Jennifer's sadness. That blue-furred jag kept coming back to his mind again and again. He wondered if it would depress or frustrate her how much of an impact she had made on the people around her. He could easily envision her angry with the fact that people actually missed her.

Before he knew it, the road ran out, terminating in an old parking lot where just a few rusted out cars resided, clearly abandoned decades ago. There didn't seem to be any signs of recent activity. They took a moment to search the cars, prying open the two trunks that were closed, and poking through the interiors of the vehicles.

"Do you ever think about before?" Jennifer asked as they searched the vehicles.

"Before the undead?" Cait asked. She nodded. "Sometimes, but not often."

"How long has it actually been?" David asked.

"I've heard forty years," Jennifer said.

"I've heard fifty, but no one seems to know for sure anymore. I guess some people say they're sure, and I lean towards believing the older people, the ones who were still actually alive. But I know that things had been pretty bad for years by the time I was even born," Cait replied.

"Same," David said, and Jennifer nodded.

"What do you think about it?" Cait asked.

"I don't know. Sometimes I wonder what it was like, because I feel like I'm just not getting it. This idea that the world was...not like this. That there were *billions* of people. That's just...I can't even imagine it. And the stories I've heard, that people went up to the *moon.* I mean...I feel like that's just nonsense, it's impossible, but then I don't know. I guess cars would sound impossible if we'd never seen any before. Or computers. Or helicopters. Maybe we did go up into outer space."

"Have you seen a helicopter?" David asked.

"Never in flight, but I've seen wrecks of helicopters and airplanes."

"I saw one that flew," Cait said. "The place

where I grew up, there was one there. They didn't use it often, it was hard to maintain, but I did see it fly. It was so weird looking. Almost like a big metal wasp or something..." she snorted. "I guess if wasps had blades for wings that spun around really, really fast."

"I've gotten the impression that there were tons of amazing things that we've just...forgotten, as a species. It does make me wonder how much we've lost. But I guess, in a way, we're at least lucky in that we grew up with the world already like this. We aren't missing much."

"There is that," Cait agreed.

"Fuck, there's nothing in here," David muttered as they finished searching the last car. He looked at the path that, at first at least, was made of metal stairs and had a railing, ascending up the side of the mountain, drifting off to the right before disappearing from view. "Well, let's get this over with," he said.

Both Cait and Jennifer made noises of agreement and trio left the parking lot and carefully began to ascend the stairway. David led the way, his movements slow and careful as although the stairs didn't seem like they were going to go anywhere, they did creak ominously. Bit by bit, they made their way up that initial incline.

The minutes passed in a chilled silence, the only sounds they had for company being the ones they made themselves and the occasional wind that whispered through the trees. Before long, they rose above the forest.

The stairs came to an end finally, letting onto an outcropping that had at one point been a scenic picnic spot. The weathered remains of four big wooden tables, the kind that came with benches attached, took up most of the space. There was a railing that had broken in several places surrounding the outcropping, complete with a few devices stuck up on metal poles. They had glass lenses built into them.

"What are these?" David murmured.

"I think they act like binoculars," Cait replied.

"Huh."

He didn't really feel like he needed binoculars honestly. They were probably a good eighty feet up in the air now and the view was spectacular. He could see a hell of a lot. He saw the river and the lake, he saw the warehouse and the watchtower, the military outpost, he even could just barely make out the campgrounds that he now called home.

"This is amazing," Jennifer whispered.

"Yes, this is quite the view," Cait agreed.

David turned around. "Come on," he said, spying a path that led up and deeper into the mountain, then curving out of sight, presumably leading to the radio tower itself. He sure hoped so. "Let's keep going–"

David froze as a shadow fell across him, and he looked up, fear suddenly entering him. It was probably just a bird, but why–

"Oh *fuck!*" he screamed, raising his pistol.

Both women immediately looked up and echoed his sentiment.

It was a hunter.

A hunter had finally come for them.

It was descending from much higher up, and for a few seconds that seemed to stretch on and on, he had a very clear view of it. It was terrifying. It was a humanoid figure covered in dark gray patches of feathers that had fallen away in random places, revealing ugly, scarred, leathery skin beneath. Wings sprouted from its back and they were enormous, though they had no feathers and were closer to those of a bat's wings than a bird's. He saw huge black claws growing from its feet and its hands, and the face that stared down at him had a horrifying combination of human and avian twisted by the virus that had mutated it.

A hunter was an AV that had been turned into an undead, the only among the inhumans who could fly, and it was possibly the most terrifying.

He had only ever seen them from a distance, and had heard many stories about them.

"Shoot it!" Cait screamed, and then opened fire. David and Jennifer immediately joined in, aiming straight up.

The bullets cut through the air and penetrated the thing's thick flesh, and blood began to rain down as it shrieked wildly. Extending its clawed feet downwards, it began to dive bomb them as it tucked its huge wings in. David kept firing as fast as he could and all three pistols converged on it, punching holes in its chest and limbs, and two got it through the head, killing it. They all dove out of the way as it crashed into the area with them.

It landed on one of the tables and smashed it utterly, reducing it to splinters.

"Oh fuck me," Cait whispered heavily as she reloaded with shaky hands, "that's a hunter. That's a fucking hunter, man. I haven't seen one of those in forever. Holy shit–"

Another shriek cut through the air, and then another.

More shadows fell across them and David stared up in terror as he hastily began to reload. A half-dozen more of the flying monsters came from around the side of the mountain and immediately started to fly straight towards them. He finished reloading, aimed up, and opened fire. Jennifer and Cait joined him.

They held their ground as they pumped lead into the flying terrors, trying to bring them down as quickly as possible. David emptied his whole magazine and managed to put three rounds through one's chest, which was apparently enough to kill it, and it spiraled out of control and disappeared, banging down the side of the mountain.

He didn't bother reloading, instead dropping his pistol and pulling out the submachine gun that he'd brought with him. Since there'd been an influx of guns after their successful assault, he was traveling places with more than just a pistol now. They all were. He waited for the pack to get a little closer, as the SMG didn't have quite the effective range as the pistol.

Cait or Jennifer managed to score a headshot on another one of them and it was smashing down the side of the mountain after the other. The remaining four split up, going in different directions, then wheeling back and coming for them. David took aim.

Once he had one of them in his sights, he cut loose, sending a spray of red hot lead directly into the body of the hunter. It was a good hit, punching straight through its broad, misshapen chest, and it killed the thing outright. Unfortunately, that meant that he now had something like four hundred pounds of monstrous bird creature falling right at him. David barely managed to throw himself out of the way before it smashed into the ground where he'd been standing, sending up a huge puff of snow and dirt.

They managed to put down all but two of them before needing to reload, and before the creatures managed to close the gap between them. One swooped and made a grab for Cait. She shouted and dodged, just barely managing to avoid its grasp. David saw its claws come within inches of grasping her.

The other landed with a heavy thud in between him and Jennifer. He stepped to the side so that he didn't accidentally shoot her, took aim, and opened fire. The hunter was fast and although it actually managed to leap to the side and avoid his shots, the movement almost looking like a twitch more than anything given its speed and reaction time, it did not, however, manage to avoid the shotgun blast that Cait delivered straight to the back of its head.

That decapitated it outright.

David and Jennifer quickly shifted their focus to the remaining hunter, which was wheeling around again, coming for them, and opened fire. David emptied his SMG and managed to clip its wings several times, and Jennifer shot it once through the neck, then again through the head, and that put it down permanently.

"Come on," David said as he hastily reloaded both of his weapons, "let's get the fuck out of here before more of them show up."

"Yeah," Cait agreed, her normally calm and even cavalier attitude clearly disrupted by the display. She looked pale and a bit shaken, as did Jennifer.

The trio finished reloading as they left the picnic area, and the next several minutes were spent hurriedly making their way up the trail, which wound back in on itself as it ascended, thankfully pointing them towards the radio tower. None of them said anything as they hiked up higher and higher.

David felt the cold air burning in his lungs as he continually scanned the skies for more signs of the hunters. But that seemed to be all of them. For now at least. Finally, after a good fifteen or so minutes of nothing but panting and hiking, they came to what appeared to be the final portion of the trail. It ended in the plateau that held the radio tower.

"Has anyone ever seen any AVs around here?" David asked. He found himself thinking about them. AVs were rare, but not as rare as squids or nymphs. Although they could fly, most of them didn't, as some people put it, 'go native', in the same way that nymphs lived in the forests or squids lived in the oceans, doing their own things. AVs tended to live among humans and reps and jags and goliaths, but he had noticed that either they were just fewer in number, or he hadn't run into all that many in his lifetime.

"I've heard of some," Cait said, "I even saw a few flying a few times over in this direction, but that was back near when I'd first arrived. For some reason, I just didn't connect that this would be a place they would hang out. But I guess it makes sense. It's a mountain, it's up high, it's secluded but has a great view of the surrounding area." She sighed heavily and scanned the skies once more. "I fucking hate those things."

"Yeah, they're so scary," Jennifer muttered.

"We can handle them," David replied. "We proved that. We can handle whatever comes our way."

"So far," Cait murmured.

He had to agree with her there, and he was sounding more confident than he really was. He still knew that all it took was one run of shitty luck and you were fucked. He'd seen too many people die from stupid accidents or dumb risks.

They reached the radio tower a few minutes later and discovered that there wasn't just a tower there, but there was also a small structure as well that looked like it had held up surprisingly decently over the decades.

"Why don't you two search the structure while I check out the tower? That's where the parts I'm looking for should be," Jennifer suggested.

"On it," David replied, hefting his SMG while Cait held her shotgun. They'd both been reluctant to put away their heavier arsenal since their run-in with the latest horrors from the undead ranks. The front door was closed and when David tried it, he found it locked. He glanced at Cait, who looked back at him, her features set.

He knocked on it a few times. "Anyone in there?!" he called.

Nothing. Just the occasional wind.

He decided to try and brute force it, as it was a wooden door and probably weak with age. He took a few running steps at it and smashed his shoulder into it. The lock gave with a loud snapping sound and the door flew inwards. David managed not to fall on his ass and instead raised his SMG, ready for something hostile to be inside.

But there was nothing, just a simple room.

Slowly, he went in, Cait right behind him, and they each covered one side of the room. Almost the entire building was made up of that room. There was just one door, and it was open, leading into a very small bathroom. The place looked relatively intact, though everything was covered in a layer of dust.

David studied it all as he looked for potential hiding places. One corner was taken up by a table occupied by radio gear that was long dead, though surprisingly intact. Another corner had a bed tucked away into it, with a little nightstand beside it. Another corner held a tiny kitchenette that was little more than a sink, a bit of counterspace, a very small refrigerator, and a wood-burning stove. He and Cait split up and began to search.

He took the kitchen area and she went into the bathroom and they worked in silence for several moments. Thoughts drifted to and fro through his head, mostly focusing on the campgrounds.

Was he actually going to be able to pull this off?

He honestly was feeling more capable than he had ever before in his entire life, and he believed in and trusted the women that were helping him, but he knew how quickly it could turn against him. What if there was a fire? Another attack? What if a sickness swept over them all, something far worse than a simple cold? What if Lima Company decided that they didn't like the competition?

Fuck, what if there was some kind of natural disaster?

He sighed softly as he saw that what food was left in here was long since rotted away and of no use at all. He finished searching the kitchen area and moved over to the bed. He poked around beneath it and saw something under there. Reaching into his pocket, he pulled out his little flashlight, turned it on, and shined it under.

"Hello," he muttered. There was a book of some kind, definitely not like the paperbacks he'd been finding for April. He retrieved it and studied it. It was bigger, and flatter, the cover a bit sturdier. **OFFICIAL LOG** was written across the front.

"What's that?" Cait asked as she emerged from the bathroom.

"Not sure." He flipped it open to the first page and found that it was filled with short sections of text broken up by empty spaces now and then, with numbers written above and to the left of each little section. "What is this?" he muttered.

Cait studied it, standing beside him. "It's log entries," she murmured. "Those are dates."

David looked over the strings of numbers. He had vague notions of things like calendars and dates, he knew that the year was broken up into months, and that was about as far as he went in telling time in a broader scale. Mostly, people just went by the seasons now. It was winter. If he had to guess, he'd say it was January.

"This first date here...oh one, twelve, two thousand twenty four. The first two numbers, I believe, are the month. The second two numbers are the day. The final four the year," she said.

"So oh one, first month of the year, that would be March."

"No, January," she said.

"Wait, what? Why would *January* be the first month of the year? It's dead in the middle of winter," he asked.

She shrugged. "I have no idea. I've always been confused about that myself. March *does* seem like the time to start a new year, it's when everything's coming back to life, usually, a time of renewal. But for some reason January is the first month of the new year. So...it looks like...this is the logbook of a...I think a soldier who was sent here to maintain the radio equipment after the world broke."

They spent a moment reading a few more entries. They were pretty dry. The person in question first wrote of the journey to get here, which sounded interesting, but the way they wrote broke everything down to the most minimal of the facts.

Attacked by undead.

Attacked by raiders.

Investigated distress call.

Found abandoned military outpost.

Shit like that. Despite this, it was an interesting read. He and Cait sat down on the bed together and began thumbing through it, though they only got through the actual journey to the radio tower before Jennifer came into the building.

"What's that?" she asked.

"A journal from like...a really long time ago. Within the first decade of the outbreak, it seems," David replied. He closed it and tucked it away into his backpack. He was definitely going to read this through in the near future. "How'd it go?"

"I found one of the parts," Jennifer replied. "Which means we'll definitely have to hit up the factory if we want to find the other."

"Great," Cait muttered. She sighed heavily and got to her feet.

"At least we got this far," David said. "Let's finish our search and go home. We're going to need to rest up if this is going to be as bad as you say it is."

"Yeah," she agreed.

They got to work.

. . .

David looked out the window at the bleak winter night and tried not to be nervous.

Honestly, he *shouldn't* be nervous about what was going to happen. He'd already been naked in a bed with Amanda, and at this point, he'd had multiple new sexual partners in the past month. He would have thought he'd have built up more confidence by now. He supposed he had, but still, that nervousness persisted. Even the thing that he thought to be nervous about, the birth control, had been covered.

After getting back from the radio tower they'd eaten lunch and then spent the rest of the day finishing repairs to the fence, sorting out supplies from the warehouse, and seeing to the needs of the two groups that they now housed, and after *that*, he'd gone over to the hospital after paranoia had finally got the best of him.

After all, he didn't want the answer to the question of 'is the birth control working' to be: *Well, I got a married woman pregnant.* He honestly should've asked about it sooner, but there was so much on his mind. Thankfully, there had been a test. Which had been fun. Katya had jacked him off until she got a sperm sample.

Studying it with some specialized thing that he didn't recognize had revealed that the birth control had worked: he couldn't get anyone pregnant for the next month. After asking Katya if she'd be okay with going to the factory with them tomorrow and getting a yes, he'd returned back home, had dinner, and run several more errands around the campground, as there was always more that needed doing.

And then, finally, the time had come for him and Amanda to meet again.

And this time they would fuck.

David heard movement downstairs. Amanda had come over after dinner and they'd all started talking and eventually she'd shooed him upstairs to get ready while she talked with his, as she put it, inner circle. Maybe that's what he was nervous about. What were they talking about down there? Him? Surely there were better things to talk about.

There was a quiet knock at the door.

"Come in," he said, turning from the window.

The door opened and Amanda slipped in. She closed it behind her and smiled at him. "You're a very lucky boy, David," she said.

"Yes," he agreed, "I definitely am."

"The ladies in your life are very nice ladies. Very fun, very friendly. We had a nice conversation. But before I could truly let time get away from me, which is very easy to do when you're in a good conversation, I knew I needed to slip up here and have some fun, because I *do* have a family I need to be there for," she said.

"I understand," he replied. "You want to get to it?"

"Yes. Let me wash really quick. I assume you did, already?"

"Yeah."

"Okay. Go get ready."

He nodded and began taking off his clothes. He wasn't sure why he'd put them back on after washing. Probably just force of habit more than anything else, or maybe paranoia. You could spring into action much more effectively when you were already clothed. He stripped down and got into the enormous custom-made bed that he and Evelyn, and often others, slept in.

He watched Amanda strip down quickly and efficiently, and soon she was nude before their washbasin, cleaning herself off just as efficiently. Within two minutes she was soaped, washed, and dried, and then she was crossing the room and climbing beneath the blankets with him.

"Hi," she said as she got up close to him, staring at him with wide, beautiful eyes.

"Hi," he murmured.

"You nervous?"

"Kind of."

"Don't be. You'll do fine. We've already been here before, remember?" she said softly, and then she leaned in and kissed him.

And then his anxiety began to melt away as they locked lips and began to touch each other. Her skin was so soft and smooth and warm. He ran his hands over her curves and her slim, fit body, groping and squeezing her gently, and felt her doing the same to his own body. He felt his lust welling up within him, his cock stiffening, his stomach beginning to boil with the dark excitement of desire.

As they continued making out and his fingertip once again found her clit and began to massage it gently, David knew that this time it was going to be his turn to provide the oral. She had done such a fantastic job sucking him off that he had to lick her clit.

"Oh!" she moaned in surprise as he started to pleasure her. "You are...good with that," she murmured, closing her eyes and biting her lower lip, focusing on the bliss.

"I've had a lot of practice just recently," he replied.

"Yes, I imagine so...between your three lovers and...mmm...and Ashley, and the others you mentioned, I imagine you've gotten good at pleasuring pussy. Ah!"

"I seem to have." He kissed her once more, then stopped, and she opened her eyes. He began to shift lower. "I've also gotten good with my tongue."

"Oh fucking hell yes," she whispered, watching as he pulled the blankets back and got down in between her thighs.

He told himself that this was just like how it went when he went down on Cait or Evie or April or Ashley, and he'd done that at least a dozen times apiece to them, probably more. He'd never really done a shitty job, he'd never failed to elicit a positive response from them. So, just like with the others.

He got to work, tonguing her clit slowly, massaging it with the tip of his tongue really, and felt her moan and shudder in response. An excellent start. As he started working her clit, licking at it, lavishing it with pleasure, it really hit him again that he was doing sexual things with a mature, married woman. That was really fucking happening.

That was a literal goddamned fantasy last month.

And now here was Amanda, writhing in pleasure on her back, about to allow him to fuck her raw and probably finish inside of her. He made a note to ask about that, because that wasn't the kind of thing you just sprang on someone.

"Oh! David!" she cried, and she bucked and he realized as he began fucking her with his fingers as he ate her out, that he had made her orgasm.

He kept going, working her pussy as best he could, wanting to give her an excellent ride. And apparently he did. She had to keep her hands over her mouth from being *too* loud. They did have more people here now, so that was something to consider. He worked her through the orgasm, and when he was done, sat up and wiped his mouth on the back of his hand, unable to keep from grinning at her.

"If you want to fuck me right now, you can," she said, keeping her pale legs open.

"Yes, ma'am," he replied as he began to crawl on top of her.

"You're sure about that birth control?" she asked.

"Yes. I went back over to the hospital today, had them run some tests. They confirmed that it was working, and I trust them to tell me the truth," he replied, pausing before entering her. "Are you still comfortable with this?"

"Yes, I trust you," she replied. "You can fuck me bareback, and you can come inside of me. I want you to appreciate this opportunity, however, as I *very* rarely let anyone I meet extra-martially do those things."

"I appreciate it so extremely much," he replied, and began to slip into her.

She moaned and a look of pleasure crawled across her face. "Fuck, yes," she whispered as he penetrated her. "That's just...yes. That feels *so* good after an intense orgasm from good oral. And you are *very* good at-*oh!*" she moaned as he pushed all the way into her.

"Thank you," he replied, and laid down on top of her.

She felt amazing inside. Slick and hot and *so* fucking good. He groaned loudly as he quickly began to lose himself inside of her wonderful, tight perfection. She reached up and grabbed him, pulling him closer to her and then kissing him. Locking lips with her as he slid into her again and again was beyond amazing. Feeling her hot, tight body against his own, her naked skin against his own, was a piece of paradise that he thought he would never get tired of.

"How does it feel?" she moaned to him as he drove into her. "How does raw, married pussy feel,

David?"

"It's so good," he panted, "so fucking good, Amanda..."

"Yes...fuck, your cock feels *really* good," she moaned, spreading her legs a bit more, then bringing them up and putting her feet in the air. "Like...*really* good. Holy shit. Ah!"

"Better than you've had in a while?" he asked, staring down at her beautiful face. She looked flushed, her hair already beginning to become a mess.

"I..." She looked guilty suddenly. "Yeah," she admitted.

"It's okay, I know how you feel," he said, and kissed her again.

"I don't know if it's just the excitement of doing it with you for the first time or the bareback or just your shape and size, but...mmm..." The pleasure overcame her face again and she shuddered. "It's so fucking good, taking your cock like this."

"Don't feel bad," he said.

"Why?"

"I've...had similar experiences," he murmured.

"Oh?" She raised an eyebrow, then moaned as he pushed deeper into her. "The best pussy you've ever had isn't downstairs?"

"No," he admitted. "I haven't told them. I don't intend to, because I don't think it matters."

"You love them," she said, "that's what matters. Your relationship is more than how good the sex is."

"Yes, and it's not even like the sex is bad. They're all great in bed in their own way."

"You're right...I love my husband, and he's great too, but...I guess that's no reason not to admit that this is the best fucking dick I've had in years..." she moaned loudly.

"Good girl," he replied, and kissed her hard on the mouth, then started fucking her faster. She cried out, grabbing at his back, and within another thirty seconds, he had her coming. She squirted and screamed as he fucked her orgasming pussy.

"Yes, David! *Yes! YES!*" she cried and he could feel her vaginal muscles convulsing and he knew he wasn't far off himself.

Her pussy might not be Ellie's, but it was *really* fucking good and he didn't care because honestly he didn't rank. Sex was sex, and in the moment it was often fucking fantastic, and this was no exception. He moaned loudly as his orgasm overtook him, bursting brightly into existence. It felt like a hot, pink light inside of him, a tremendous energy, a warmth that began to fill him as he in turn started to fill Amanda was his seed.

He started coming into her pussy, filling up that sweet, married vagina one, hard pump at a time, his cock jerking, contracting, twitching madly as he came along with her. They came together and it was a perfect union of bliss.

Some time later, they were both left sweaty and panting, holding each other closely, him still inside of her.

"My," she whispered, still trembling occasionally. "That was...very good. I thought you would be a decent lay, but I didn't think it would be like *that*. Fuck."

"Uh-huh," he managed.

After a bit, he pulled out of her, and she sat up. "Oh," she said, looking down. "They were right."

"What?"

"Your girlfriends. They warned me that you came a lot. Like, a lot. That's apparently true. You came a lot."

"How do you feel about that?" he asked.

She got up and moved back over to the washbasin. "I think there might be some merit to the idea that the more you come the more turned on you were. In my experience, that's true. Of course that doesn't necessarily count for how long it's been since you last came. But I'll take it as a compliment. You did seem very into me."

"I've been into you since I first saw you," he replied.

She laughed. "The first time you saw me I was recovering from nearly dying."

"And you were *still* crazy hot," he said.

"Well thank you, David." She finished cleaning herself up, then began to pull her clothes back on. "I have to go now, but...can this be at least a semi-regular thing? Because I *really* enjoyed that. I don't want it to get *too* regular, but...once a week? Twice a month?" she asked.

"Whatever you feel most comfortable with," he replied.

"You're so easy to work with. Okay. I'll think about it and let you know." She came over and crouched by the bed where he still lay, then gave him a kiss. "You were a great lay."

"You, too," he replied.

She left and headed downstairs. A few moments later, the door opened and Cait, Evie, April, and Jennifer all came in.

"So that sounded fun," Cait said, crawling onto the bed with him.

"Yes, it was very fun," he replied. "How are you all?"

"Horny," Evie said.

"Yeah," Jennifer murmured, rubbing her arm, a curious mixture of lust and shyness on her face.

"Well, I'm sure there's something we can do about that," Cait said.

"I'll need a minute," David said.

"You get one," Evie said as she began taking her shirt off.

CHAPTER EIGHT

This time around, David was feeling less confident.

He wasn't sure why and had been thinking on it all the way to the hospital, which was their first stop for the day. He'd had very great sex last night and this morning, he'd had a good breakfast, and nothing bad had happened in the night.

It was probably, he finally decided, the sky. It looked ominous, covered from horizon to horizon in miserable gray clouds. A cold, restless wind was scouring the landscape, biting into them, slicing through their clothes. It was making conversation difficult, so they'd hardly shared a word on the way there.

The plan was set, at least. They would go to the hospital first and pick up Katya. Provided nothing had happened and she was still set to go with them. Even without her, he felt decently confident. He had Cait, Evie, and Jennifer with him and they were all capable in their own ways. And he'd gotten good at survival, or so it seemed to him at least. He knew he wasn't at Cait's level, and wasn't sure he ever would be, but he could get by. Although he had to admit, they were doing a lot more dangerous stuff nowadays.

There was a difference between surviving out in the wilderness, and intentionally going into a very dangerous location.

A big difference.

He decided to try and strike up another conversation as they continued making their way to the hospital. "So, do you think we've got this?" he asked, and then stopped talking, because that wasn't exactly what he'd meant to ask.

"What, the factory?" Cait replied. "Probably."

"No, the campgrounds. Running a village."

"Oh."

No one spoke for a few moments.

"I think you're all doing a really good job, but I've also lived by myself a lot, so I don't really know if I'd be the best judge," Jennifer offered.

"Everyone's safe and happy, for the most part, and fed, and busy," Cait said. "I think that means we're doing a good job for now. The problem is that this shit can turn sour in an instant. I think most of village running is the day-to-day shit, making sure it stays going smoothly, and the rest of it is preparing for the inevitable disaster that's looming on the horizon."

"That makes sense," Evie said. "Right now, the schedules I've written up *seem* to be working. We're already working on a decent store of firewood, although that's changing because of the influx of people. Same for the food and water. I'm glad we kept storing water over that two week period. It definitely helped. I guess the problem with something like this is that it isn't really an 'okay, I've got that taken care of' kind of goal. It's a continual goal. You can't just be good at running a village, you have to *keep* being good at it. But as for whether or not we've got this? Obviously I want to say yes, but we haven't faced a serious crisis yet, have we?"

"I don't know, our last village burned down," David replied.

"I guess so. It was a crisis and we faced it, but it's not the same. We didn't face that crisis *as village leaders,* is my point," Evie said.

"I think we'll do better when something like that

happens," Cait murmured. "I think the difference between us and them is that our village is more...connected. We're more of a community and less of a group of people living together. We know each other, we care about each other. I'm hoping that it extends to all the new people we've gathered so far. They all seem pretty on the level, though, at least."

The hospital was up ahead. They fell silent as they made their final approach on it. Before they could get to the front door, it opened up and Katya stepped out. She was done up in her gear, apparently ready and raring to go with them.

"So...you're ready, I take it?" David asked.

"Fuck yes, I am. I'm more than ready to get on with this," she replied.

"Well, okay then," Cait said, and they set off from the hospital.

"How is everyone?" Evie asked.

"Good. Vanessa's getting impatient again. I had to talk her out of going on this particular expedition, although honestly if you were going somewhere less dangerous, I think she'd be up to the task," Katya replied.

"Maybe we can take her with us to the construction site," David murmured.

"What, the one in the valley?"

"Yeah."

"Yeah, I could see that."

"I understand you sampled my boyfriend," Evie said after they'd fallen silent for a few moments.

"I did indeed. He was quite a fine fuck," Katya replied.

"Seems to be a lot of that recently," Cait murmured.

"What, you fuck someone else new?" Katya

154

asked.

"He slept with a married woman last night."

Katya glanced at him with a raised eyebrow. "She had permission, it's an open marriage," he said defensively.

"I wasn't judging," Katya replied. "I'd be a hypocrite."

"You've cheated?" Evie asked.

"You have to be in a relationship to cheat. No, I've...found men, and women, in certain situations, and alleviated their situation," she replied.

"What's *that* supposed to mean?" Cait asked.

"It means that I've found guys and girls in relationships where their significant other didn't want to have sex with them, and I did want to have sex with them."

"You ever get caught?" David asked.

"Three times. I almost died the third time. This woman nearly blew my fucking head off. After that I decided maybe I should be a little more discreet."

"Mmm-hmm," Evie murmured.

"You don't approve."

"I can't say that I do, honestly. But I guess I can't really say much, because I don't know. Maybe the situations called for it. It's easy to look at a relationship and say, 'well, if you're going to cheat, you should just break up,' because it's often so much more complicated than that."

"That is true," Katya agreed.

They pressed on as the conversation trailed off, continuing through the dead, frozen forest. The winds picked up again, whistling through the trees, providing a haunting, discordant melody. Eventually, the trees gave way once more and the view opened up significantly. They got out onto a path that ran parallel to the lake, which stood huge and mostly frozen. David saw the fishing village as they walked by.

He wondered how they were doing. He hadn't really had a chance to visit since the last time he'd been there. Was Ruby okay? That slim, silent jag with the curiously flat demeanor and amazing skill with a rifle had been wounded the last time they'd seen her, and she had also been instrumental in the assault on the thieves.

At some point, he was going to have to go back there.

Maybe, if they cracked open the bunker and there was an absolute shitload of supplies in there, they could go on a goodwill mission and share some of the supplies with the other groups in the region. That would be the smart thing to do, he thought. Independence was great and all, but it was better to be able to rely on people, and for people to want to help you.

They kept following the path until it forked and then they took a left, following a second path, this one narrower and more overgrown, that curved around the far edge of the lake. In the distance, he could see the factory. It was a dark, ominous brick of a building that seemed to lurk among its own collection of dead trees, like it was waiting for them. He couldn't see anything moving around it, but that didn't mean anything.

There were a lot of places to hide in the wilderness, even during winter.

"I don't suppose you know anything about this place that we don't?" Cait asked Katya.

"No," she replied. "I steered clear of this place for the most part. Always gave me a bad feeling. I think me and Vanessa might've gotten around to it eventually, though."

"Well, hopefully it isn't too much trouble," Cait murmured.

"If it is, we're ready," Katya said, and she sounded pretty confident.

David hoped she was right.

They walked without incident along the path to the factory. David couldn't help but study the scenery. It looked like some of the paintings he'd seen during his exploration of this post-apocalyptic landscape, or some of the old framed photographs that had survived. Winter was bleak, but there was definitely a stark sort of beauty to a snow-swept environment. Though he still would prefer to be enjoying the view from inside of a heated building. It was goddamned cold today. The factory grew closer and closer until finally they found themselves standing at its base, staring up at it from an empty parking lot.

"I don't see any vipers around," Katya murmured softly. "I thought there'd be some here, given our proximity to the lake."

"They could be hiding, or inside the structure," David replied.

"Yeah. We should search the perimeter first," Cait said, and David nodded in agreement.

They stuck together, keeping in a loose formation as they struck off to the right and started to make their way slowly around the outside of the building. It was just more of the same on the other side: dead trees, frozen earth, the occasional bit of trash laying around, and cold winds blowing. They cleared one side, then another, and yet another. They came back to their starting point and had still encountered no enemies.

They'd also discovered two entrances, and both of them were rusted shut so firmly that it would take a welding torch to get them open.

"So now what?" Evie asked unhappily.

Cait was looking up. David followed her gaze and frowned. There was a fire escape on this side of the building. It looked pretty old and rickety.

"No," Evie said.

"I don't think we have a choice," Jennifer muttered.

"There *has* to be another way, it looks so dangerous..."

"We *need* the part, and I'm not sure where else to look."

"I'll do it," Cait said.

"No," David said immediately, and stepped closer to her.

"David, you can't stop me from doing dangerous things just because..." She looked down briefly, laying a hand over her stomach.

"Cait," he said, and she looked up at him, "if I fall, and break my arm, then that sucks. But I'll heal up. If *you* fall, and something happens..." He laid his own hand gingerly over hers. "If something happens to our baby, then..." He wasn't sure how to finish the sentence.

"Okay," she whispered. "You're right." Some of the steel came back into her blue eyes. "But this doesn't mean I'm giving it *all* up, David. I'm still going to need to do dangerous things sometimes," she said firmly.

"I know," he replied. "But if I can take the risk, or someone else can, then–"

"Then I'll pass it along," she said with a sigh. "This is just a sacrifice I need to make sometimes. I know, goddamnit. But I *hate* the thought of you or Evie or anyone else taking a risk on my behalf. I hate it."

"It's what we do, Cait," he replied. "We suffer for each other, because we love each other. Because sometimes that's what's required in a relationship."

She sighed heavily. "Especially in a relationship where we're living *this* fucking life," she muttered.

He laughed, and kissed her. She kissed him back hard. "Come back to me safe, do you fucking understand me?"

"Yes, love," he replied. "I will." He looked over at the others and realized they had stepped a little away, to give him and Cait some privacy, although Evie was watching them both closely, perhaps looking to intervene if need be. Jennifer and even Katya looked a little uncomfortable.

"Come on, Jennifer. Evie, you're going to boost us up there. Me first, and when I say it's safe, then Jennifer. Sound good?" he asked.

"Yes," Evie replied.

They walked over to the fire escape. As he came to stand beneath it, staring up at the rusty metal, David felt his confidence start to slip away. It looked pretty fucking rickety. The ladder that would be granting them access under optimum conditions had broken off and was nowhere to be seen. There was still a bit of it hanging off, and it was going to have to do.

"Okay, Evie," he said, making sure his weapons were secure, "help me up."

"Be careful, honey," she replied as she laced her fingers together.

"I will. Love you. Love you, Cait," he said.

They both told him that they loved him, as well,

and then Evie boosted him up. With her seven and a half foot height, she managed to get him up without a problem. He grabbed onto the broken ladder and hauled himself up. He clambered up onto the platform and waited, listening to it creak and groan as it shuddered briefly beneath him. He waited for it to come tumbling down, every muscle in his body tensing, but it didn't. It held. He let out a long, slow sigh of relief, then started walking.

He ascended the fire escape slowly, picking up speed as he realized that it was actually more stable than it looked. He tried to look into some of the windows as he passed by, but they were all surprisingly intact and extremely filthy, as opaque as the metal the building was made of. Within a few minutes, he'd reached the roof and found it empty.

"Okay, come up," he called down.

"Coming up," Jennifer replied.

He watched as Evie boosted her up. She grabbed the ladder just as he had and within seconds she was following his path. While she came up, he searched around the roof, quickly checking behind a few of the larger pieces of machinery sticking up out of it. Air conditioners, he realized after a bit. And ventilation pieces. There was nothing up there, and he managed to find a hatch by the time Jennifer had made it up.

"I found a way in," he said, waving her over.

She quickly joined him, looking around nervously. "Have you seen anything?"

"No, nothing," he replied as he began prying open the hatch. It took a minute of effort and Jennifer's help, but they got it open. As they did, David shined his flashlight down inside. A room, some dusty shelves, and a few moldy boxes waited below. "Wait here," he said, and moved back over to the others. "We've found a way in and it looks clear so far, we're going in."

"Okay, we'll...be waiting here, I guess," Cait said.

"Maybe I should come up there, too," Katya said.

"It *would* be nice to have some backup," David replied after a moment.

"Okay, go on ahead without me, I'll start coming up," she said.

"Thanks." He wasn't sure why he hadn't considered that. Maybe he was getting used to trying to put as few people at risk as possible, and just take all the risks himself. Well, that probably wasn't a very smart way to be, but he'd seen so much suffering, so much pain and misery, that he was finding it difficult to tolerate the thought of any more being visited upon them.

But that was life, wasn't it?

He rejoined Jennifer and then climbed down a ladder he found bolted to the wall beneath the hatch. It held steady and he was delivered into a small storage room. The air was thick and seemed to close in around him as he scanned the area more thoroughly with his flashlight, keeping his pistol in his other hand, hoping that something wasn't lurking among the shadows. It was a small room, and although he didn't see or even sense anything in the room with him but Jennifer as she came down the ladder, he could smell their scent on the air.

"Come on," he whispered, moving over to the door and opening it quietly.

Or trying to, anyway, its hinges squealed as he opened it up and he winced, gritting his teeth as he finished opening it. A hallway waited beyond the doorway, and it was about as dark out there. He aimed his pistol and flashlight to the right, seeing more hallway and more doors, and a lot of windows directly across from him, then the other direction, seeing more of the same. The hallway seemed clear.

He walked into it and over to the windows. Peering through the nearest one, he saw that the factory was set up roughly similar to the warehouse he'd found Robert's group in.

He was on a second story overlooking a huge, open space, though the difference here was that the space was not filled with crates, but machinery. Old, rusted out hulks of machinery. There were a lot of shadows down there. As he stared at the factory floor, he thought he saw something move. David shifted the light towards the source of the movement, waiting as Jennifer came up behind him. She silently joined him at the window.

"What?" she whispered finally.

"Thought I saw something," he murmured. "Where's this part you'll need?"

She sighed unhappily. "It'll be down there, in one of the machines."

"Of course," he said. "Come on, then. I think–" He had begun to bring the flashlight away, but then he saw something else and this time he was positive he'd seen movement. He stepped closer to the window and readjusted the flashlight.

"I saw it, too," Jennifer whispered.

"Maybe we should–"

Something screamed wildly, terrifyingly close, and suddenly a dark, clawed hand came down from above and smashed through the window. Both of them screamed and fell back in different directions.

David watched in horror as a ripper climbed in through the broken-open window. He dropped his flashlight and took aim, then started firing off shots. Three went wild, but finally the fourth shot connected and caught it right in the head. It went slack like a ragdoll, began to fall out of the window, and instead got snagged on the glass.

From all around them, all across the factory, a chorus of wild screaming and shrieking sounded. It was like the whole building was coming alive.

"Fuck! Fuck!" he snapped as more windows were smashed out. "You cover that way!"

"Okay!" Jennifer replied.

Out the nearest window, he could see more rippers, a lot more rippers coming out of the machinery. And, shit, some of them burst through the open doorways in the hallway with him, the nearest one barely ten feet away. He aimed and opened fire on it first, putting two shots into its chest and spraying its dark blood across the wall behind it. There were already three more in the hallway and they were rushing at him. As he took aim, he heard Jennifer firing away behind him, and more glass shattering.

He heard Katya shout something from above but he didn't have time to respond. At least they were going to have backup.

He began squeezing the trigger and emptied his pistol putting down two of the three rippers running for him with claws out and mouths open, slobbering and shrieking. He wounded the third, stalling it long enough to hastily toss out the spent magazine and shove a new one in. He barely got the gun aimed in time as another two rippers climbed into the hallway through broken windows, and more were on the way.

David kept firing, his heart hammering away inside his chest, threatening to break through his ribcage as he fought for control. One shot into the mouth of the nearest ripper, blowing part of its head off, then the next shot missed, the next after that taking one in the shoulder. He took advantage of its stumble and put two bullets in its chest and another in its neck. It was down, but now there were *four more* in the fucking hallway!

He emptied the pistol again and then shoved it into the holster and brought his submachine gun to bear.

"All right, fuckers!" he screamed as now six of the rippers were in the hallway.

He leveled the gun at them and opened fire.

The gunfire tore up the corridor and began punching into their sleek, dark bodies. The muzzle flare made them look like still images, like dark demons rapidly encroaching on him, almost like they were teleporting closer with each passing second. One went down, then two and three, the fourth stumbled backwards and toppled over. His gun clicked empty as the fifth one took a shot to the forehead and flopped back.

As he reloaded, he was horrified to see that the numbers he'd just put down were already being replaced! And Jennifer was shouting and firing behind him, not being able to let up at all apparently. Where was Katya?!

As he thought it, he suddenly sensed motion at his back and she appeared at his side with a pistol out. He finished reloading in that instant and they both opened fire. This time the rippers were cut down twice as fast. Katya was a fast and terribly accurate shot. Every time she squeezed the trigger, it was a headshot.

David emptied a second magazine and as he went

to reload, suddenly realized that no more were climbing in through the broken windows now. Katya put down the final two that were still in there with them and immediately turned around and went to help Jennifer. David finished reloading, then went to the windows to check for reinforcements. He retrieved his flashlight with a huff of irritation and then shined it down there.

He didn't see anything else moving.

The gunfire finally died off behind him.

"Well...holy shit," Katya said after a few silent seconds.

"Goddamn, fuck that," David growled, panting. "Jesus fucking...Jennifer, go back and tell them that we're okay."

"Uh...y-yeah," she replied. "Yeah."

"Are you okay?" he asked.

"I'll be okay," she replied, though she was clearly shaken.

He was too. He watched her go, then looked at Katya. She seemed pretty calm, maybe a little excited even. "Help me search these rooms," he said.

She nodded, and they set to work.

...

They spent an hour in that miserable, wretched, dark place.

Only three good things came out of it. The first was that Jennifer finally found her part. Once they'd cleared out the area, Katya had stuck with her, providing her protection and watching over her while she began searching through the machinery. The second was that David managed to gather a backpack's worth of medical supplies and food, and a few books, as he searched whatever rooms he could find.

The third was that they seemed to have exhausted their supply of rippers, though this wasn't necessarily something he could enjoy in the moment, because he didn't know that the whole time they were in there. He lived in fear, every moment that they were in the dark and dead factory, that another ripper would leap out at him from the shadows, or that more of them would attack Katya and Jennifer.

Only after they were back outside and making their way slowly down the fire escape to the others did he reflect on the fact that they'd made it out alive and relatively unscathed. Though obviously Jennifer was still shaken up.

They spoke very little as they made the trek back towards the hospital.

When they arrived, they gathered out in front of it. "So, uh...now what?" Katya asked, looking around at them. She seemed the least affected by the events in the factory.

"I guess, um, I need to go back to my place, start fixing the device," Jennifer murmured. She looked up suddenly at David and Cait. "Will you go with me? You can drop me off there, I just...don't want to walk back alone."

"Yeah, we can do that," David said. "You good to stay here?" he asked Evie.

"Yes. I can use it as an opportunity to get to know the people here," she replied.

"Okay, we'll be back," Cait replied.

They said their goodbyes and then the three of them headed back into the forest again. For several minutes they walked along in silence, following the path that was becoming familiar. Eventually, Jennifer, who seemed to be in her own world, spoke up.

"I'm sorry," she said.

"What?" David asked, unsure if he'd actually heard her correctly.

"I'm sorry," she repeated. "I feel like I'm becoming a pain in the ass and like you're only tolerating me because of my technical knowledge, which is, I mean, that's fair! I mean, you don't *have* to like me–"

"Jennifer," Cait said, reaching out and taking her hand, making her stop. David stopped along with them. "We like you. Of course we like you. We aren't just tolerating you, Jennifer."

"I'm sorry," she whispered. "I'm not a fighter, not like you two, and I know it's a pain to have to watch out for me..."

"Jennifer," Cait said, and she hugged her suddenly. "What's wrong?" she asked finally.

"I'm scared," she admitted after a few seconds.

"Of what?"

"That...I'm going to lose you. You two have been...*very* good to me. And I *really* like the both of you, and Evie and April too, but for a long time, Ellie was my only real friend out here, and she just disappeared like that, and I should have seen it coming, or been better prepared for it, but it's just left me terrified, because I don't know if I could stand to have you two ripped away from me now that you're in my life, treating me so kindly..."

"Jennifer, we aren't going to abandon you," Cait said. "We're pretty committed to this place. And if for some reason we *had* to leave, you would be more than welcome to join us."

"Really?" she murmured after a bit.

David stepped up to her and rested his hands on

her hips. "Yes, Jennifer," he said. "You are our friend. We care about you. You aren't a burden, you aren't just a tool we are using and then are going to discard as soon as you become inconvenient. You matter to us. We aren't going to abandon you, Jennifer."

"Thank you," she whispered after a long moment of silence. She hugged Cait fiercely, then as soon as she let go of her, she turned and hugged David in much the same manner. He hugged her back, holding her slim, cold body tightly against his own.

"It's okay," he whispered.

"I actually believe you," she murmured. She stepped back and then looked down. "Thank you for...indulging me."

"Listening isn't indulging, Jennifer. It's what friends do," Cait said, reaching up and brushing some of the hair out of her face.

"It's been a while since I've had that in my life," she murmured.

"I know. But you have it now. If you ever want to talk, about anything, please come to us. We'll talk, we'll listen," Cait replied.

"I-I appreciate it." She sighed and shook her head. "Come on, I need to get home. I feel better now, and I just want to fix that device."

"Okay," David said.

And they set off once again.

It didn't take much longer to reach Jennifer's lonely house out in the middle of the forest. They checked around the outside to see if anything was hanging around, and then took some time to help her make sure nothing had gotten into the house while they'd been out. As they did, he noticed that Jennifer seemed down.

He thought that getting home would have cheered her up, but then he quickly remembered what she'd told them the last time they'd come here, that she had thought the same thing, and instead just found herself waiting for them to come back. After they made sure the place was secure, they gathered back in the living room.

"So, you're good to stay here and fix the tool?" David asked.

"Yeah, I'll get to work on it. When do you think you'll be back?" she asked.

"I'm not sure. It's still pretty early in the day, but I don't know how long it'll take to walk down to that construction site, search it, and get back," he admitted. "I mean, we *will* come back. How long do you think it'll take you to fix it?"

She sighed. "I'm not sure. Honestly, I need to take the whole thing apart, clean it, and put it back together again with the replacement parts. It's old and in sorry shape. But I'm almost positive I'll be able to have it done today."

"Okay then. Well, we'll be back as soon as we can, but we'll stop by the hospital first. If you finish up early and get lonely, you could go there to wait for us. They like you over there," Cait said, smiling at her.

"Do they?" Jennifer asked uncertainly.

"Obviously Vanessa does," David murmured.

She laughed. "Okay, yeah, I mean, *she* does."

"They like you, Jennifer," Cait said, then leaned in and gave her a kiss.

The effect it had on her was visible, she paused and shuddered, like it brought her whole world to a stop. He thought some of it had to do with the fact that it was Cait doing the kissing, he often felt the same way when his redhead goddess of a girlfriend kissed him, but he also thought it had to do with the fact that she was a wraith, and had lived so long in either isolation or hostility.

"We like you, too," David said as he hugged and kissed her.

"I like you both a lot," she murmured after the kiss. She cleared her throat and stepped back. "I'll, uh, get to work."

"So will we," he said.

She saw them out, staring at them for a moment before closing and locking the front door. For several moments, he and Cait walked through the snow, retracing their steps back through the path. David found his mind focusing on Jennifer, on what she had done for them, on what little he knew of her life, of her in general, of their time together.

"Cait..." he said.

"Yes?" she replied.

"Maybe we should offer to let Jennifer stay with us."

"I think that's a great idea," she replied immediately. He glanced at her. "I've been thinking the same thing, honestly. I've been thinking it for a little bit, but I wasn't sure I should even bring it up. I mean, besides space constraints, I thought she really liked having her own place and being separate from everyone else. But now that doesn't seem true at all. I think she was forced to live alone, and she made herself like it, or thought she liked it, but now that she's actually around people who are nice to her and want her around and..." she grinned impishly, "and fuck her, well, now she's remembering that she actually really likes being around people."

"That makes sense," David murmured. "Where

would we put her? As much as I think she'd agree to it, and as much as I think she misses people, I think she will want her own space that she doesn't have to share with anyone else."

Cait thought about it. "What about that place full of tables and chairs next to the kitchen, you know, where we fucked that one time?"

"'Where we fucked that one time', boy does that describe a lot of places," David replied.

She snorted and rolled her eyes. "You know what I'm talking about!"

"Yes, I know. It's a little small..."

"Yeah, but we don't have a lot of options. I don't think we could afford to give her her own cabin, it would be too nepotistic, you know? We can't be giving her special treatment just because she fucks us and we're close friends."

"To be fair, she *would* be providing a service that I don't think anyone else can with her technical knowledge. But I think she wouldn't take a cabin to herself even if we offered, she'd feel too guilty. No...we'll work something out," David replied. He let out his breath in a long sigh and shivered, watching it foam on the air. "Fuck, it's bullshit cold out."

"Yeah, we should hurry up and get this over with. I want to be home, by a fire, with you inside of me," Cait said.

"I really want that, too," he agreed.

They picked up the pace heading back towards the hospital.

CHAPTER NINE

"There, do you see it?" Vanessa asked, pointing.

David looked. They were now standing at the exact same place he and Ellie had stood not all that long ago when they were scouting the thieves out. He, Cait, Evie, and Vanessa stood atop the edge of the valley and looked into its vast, snow-covered splendor. And he saw what she was talking about: a way down to the valley floor.

"Yes," he said, nodding.

"It's secure. I've been down there a few times," Vanessa said. "Although I didn't get a chance to make it around to the construction site. Too many stalkers."

"I don't see any movement down there," Cait murmured.

"Yeah, this was before winter set in. Maybe they've died or moved on, or maybe they're just hiding. Either way, we'll be ready for them," Vanessa said, hefting the machine gun she'd brought with her.

David glanced at her. He had to admit, he was really impressed. She'd healed up quickly since last he'd seen her. When they'd gone back to the hospital and started preparing for this trip, he'd asked her if she was really up to it, and she'd admitted that sometimes she just got lazy and felt like laying around.

She wasn't always desperate to go like Katya, and getting shot a few times was a great excuse to lay around, even though she'd mostly healed up by then. He thought it was a curious thought process, but then again, people thought in different ways.

Plus, he knew how she felt. Sometimes he

wanted to just fuck off and lay around and not have to deal with anyone or anything.

Now she looked like a warrior deity, done up in snow gear with her assault rifle, submachine gun hanging off her shoulder, and pistols sitting in holsters on her huge hips. She towered over all of them, even Evie.

"No sense standing around then," Cait said, and set off.

They followed after her and for several minutes, the group walked along in relative silence, first making their way along the exterior of the area overlooking the valley, towards the trail that would ultimately take them to its floor.

"How's Jennifer?" Vanessa asked.

"She's good. She's a little anxious, and realizing that she actually likes people, or remembering it, but she's pretty happy, I think," Cait replied.

"You like her," Evie said.

"I do," Vanessa agreed. "I had a lot in common with her, I think. I know what it is to be an outcast. I know what it is to have people hate you and fear you in equal turns. Jennifer is a very good person, and she doesn't give herself enough credit." She glanced at David. "She seems particularly fond of you, it seems."

"Is she?"

"Oh yes. She spoke of you a lot during our time together. She has the worst crush on you. Though I imagine you have been fucking her during the past few days?"

"We both have," Cait murmured.

"Good. She deserves good sex."

"We all do," Evie said, and they all murmured in agreement.

They walked until they found the path, and as they began to make their way down it, he found that it was indeed very solid. You could drive a car down the path, all the way down to the valley floor. So at the very least *that* part of the trip was taken care of. Now it was a matter of actually getting there, finding valuable items, *not* finding, or at least finding and killing, any undead monsters, or dealing with people who might be there, and hauling that shit back up and out. But it was worth it, he told himself, as he had been telling himself repeatedly over the past several days as he marched relentlessly across the frozen landscape.

It was worth it.

This was helping people, and that was worth it.

As they made their way down to the bottom of the valley, it became eerily quiet. Either the winds had died down, or they just weren't reaching them down here. It was nice, either way, but it helped to create a very ominous atmosphere.

Everything was very still down on the valley floor. As they reached it, the only sounds that of their boots crunching in the snow and their breathing, they slowed to a halt and checked the immediate area. It was fairly open, though further on there were thick stands of trees here and there, and a creek, completely frozen over, cut through the middle of the valley, wandering lazily down it.

"I don't see anything," David said finally.

"Neither do I," Vanessa murmured.

"We should keep going," Cait said.

They waited a little longer to see if anything came out at them from the trees, and then they started pressing back, deeper into the valley. He could somewhat see the construction site through the random collection of trees in their path. It looked as it had from above: a frozen, skeletal structure of rusted out metal girders and the tattered remnants of what might have been canvas hanging off of it like a dead skin.

As they walked on, heading into the trees, he couldn't help but think of the factory and the rippers, the way they had been hidden among the environment. That was so true of everywhere he seemed to go nowadays.

Before, if something like the factory had happened to him, David thought that he'd be down and out for a few days at least, maybe even the rest of the week. Just call it quits for a week, because that had scared the absolute fucking shit out of him. And yet, here he was, going into another potentially lethal situation in the same day.

Was that good or bad?

Part of him thought it was really good, he was learning how to push himself, how to endure, how to be someone like, well, a leader. On the other hand, he wondered if he'd go too far in the other direction, force himself to keep pushing, keep going, and ultimately end up getting himself killed because he'd overestimated his own abilities. He'd seen people do that, insisting that they weren't weak.

David wondered if he was weak, if he really had what it took to do this.

So far, it seemed that he did, but how long would that hold up? He felt like he'd learned something important, crucial even, over the past few weeks, and it was: you could always do more. He could be preparing more, in several different ways. Storing food, gathering weapons, building alliances, all of this was crucial, but he also needed to really buckle down and start working on himself, on his own body.

Given his lifestyle, he was decently fit, he supposed, but he'd never really gone out of his way to give himself any kind of training. David hadn't lived his life with much in the way of intention, and only now was he realizing this.

He needed to be working out every day, training every day, practicing every day. Getting better with his aim, with hand-to-hand combat, his reflexes, his endurance. Two things he was really picking up on were: your greatest resource was time, and your greatest tool was your own body, including your mind. He needed to invest more time and more consistency into building himself, because it felt like right now, he was getting by on luck, whatever skill he'd managed to scrape together so far, and the people around him.

He wanted, perhaps needed, to be someone who provided rescue, not someone who got rescued.

They came out of the sparse collection of trees and into the huge clearing that held the partially constructed building. Now that they were on the valley floor, David saw that he'd actually missed that there were two other structures. They were basically copies of the trailers that he'd found Lindsay's group at, and they were pretty intact.

He took it all in as they stood at the edge of the clearing. Dead ahead of them was the partially constructed building. It didn't look like it was going to hold anything of use, but that might not be true, when they'd abandoned building it, they'd managed to lay the foundation, the metal skeleton, and a few feet of brickwork, so something could be hidden away in there. To the far left, at the edge of the clearing, obscured by some trees, were the trailers. To the far right, however, was a big, giant rock wall that had a big, giant hole in it.

And it wasn't just any cave, there were signs that this had once been a mine. The entrance was reinforced by old girders, and an ancient pickup truck lay rusting half in shadow just inside of it. He thought he might even see the remains of mining tools scattered around.

"I didn't know there was a mine down here," Evie said quietly.

"Me neither," Vanessa murmured. "Shit. At least we don't have to go in there."

"Yeah," David said. "Although..."

"Although *what?*" Vanessa asked.

"I bet no one's been in there for years, decades maybe. Maybe even since the beginning. Who knows what kind of resources are in there?" he murmured.

"Maybe," Cait said, "but we're not ready for something like that. Not even close."

"Yeah," he replied.

They set off across the clearing then, making steady progress towards the partially constructed building. They made it about halfway there before a dozen figures abruptly burst into the clearing. Some came from the mine opening, some from the trees around them. They were all making a mad dash for them, kicking up snow as they ran.

Stalkers.

"Shit," David snapped, raising his pistol.

The others stepped up beside him, spreading out a bit to give each other room, and began opening fire. As he targeted one of the stalkers and put three shots into it, he kept expecting more of them to emerge from the trees, for dozens upon dozens of them to join the initial pack. But as the seconds went by and the four of them eliminated the stalkers, no more appeared. No great chorus of shrieks rose up, no dozens of corrupted, twisted nymphs came at them. There was nothing, and the silence returned as the last echoes of the gunshots died away.

David let out his breath slowly and reloaded his pistol.

"Why are there so fucking many of these assholes?" Cait muttered.

"They were in the mine," David said softly.

"Come on," Vanessa said, setting off. "Let's get this done before more of them show up."

David nodded, holstered his pistol, and hurried off after her with Cait and Evie in tow.

They were hesitant and paranoid as they got to the partially constructed building, but as time went on and nothing happened to them, the quartet soon settled into their work. There wasn't much of anything inside the building, just some remnants of tables and tools that were so rusted as to almost be unrecognizable, as well as a few corpses that were in much the same condition. After that, they pulled open one of the trailers and as they got inside, they found...

"Jackpot," Cait said as she pulled open one of the couple of dozen crates stored inside. "Building materials. We can absolutely use this shit to fix up the cabins."

"Oh thank God," David muttered. "Although...how are we going to get this all up?"

"That's a great question," Veronica said.

"We'll find a way," Cait replied. "For now, let's keep sorting through it and see what's useful and what isn't."

They kept looking, finding roofing material,

wood, tools, nails and screws, even some windows. For a while, David was genuinely worried about how they were going to haul this stuff up and out. Even with two goliaths and all their strength, there was a lot more than they could reasonably carry. But they managed to find their solution in the second trailer.

"Now *this* is what I'm talking about," Cait said as she walked out of the trailer. She'd gone in first and declared that she had found something crucial.

It was a…

"Is that a sled?" David asked.

"Closer to a sledge, but yes. There's another one in there," she said, grunting with effort as she dragged it out onto the ground. David studied it. It was basically a big wooden sled with ropes in surprisingly good condition attached to it.

"We can't fit all the shit on it, but we can make a great haul. I think, if we pack it right, we could get half the shit here. There isn't nearly as much in the other trailer. Just some bunks and counterspace," she said.

"Perfect," David said.

They set to work after that, hauling the other sledge out and then searching the second trailer thoroughly. It looked like someone had been through at some point or another, as the cabinets were cleared out. They only managed to find a few tools. When that was finished, they started hauling the crates out onto the sledges.

They were, at least, easy to move and neatly packed. They managed to get half the crates packed up onto the sledges and tied down tightly, and then emptied another two of them of supplies that could be fitted into backpacks, which David and Cait took. Once they were all loaded down with supplies and the sledges were properly packed, they began to head back up, with Evie and Vanessa hauling the sledges.

It was much slower going heading back, but David found that even with the extra weight and slow progress, he didn't really mind. Finding the supplies had improved his mood tremendously. They had their construction needs taken care of now. They could reinforce the fence *and* fix up the cabins, not just the ones that were in dire need of repair, but even the ones that just had more inconvenient problems.

From what he could see, they were making good progress on their water and firewood supply, or at least would be, as they appeared to be outpacing their needs. And they had security in good hand now that they had both more people to help stand guard and fight if need be, but also that surplus of guns from the raid.

That left power and food.

Ideally, both would be in the bunker that Jennifer was going to crack open very soon. There could be nothing in there, but even if it was a total bust, they had made serious progress. But even as he thought this, he wondered if he was just deluding himself. Sure, it *looked* like serious progress, but what if he was missing something huge?

What if there was some tremendous, terrible tragedy looming on the horizon of the near future like a tidal wave? He supposed that was the truth of life, one of them anyway: you couldn't know the future, only try and find some combination of living your life to the fullest while also preparing for the eventual disaster that was headed your way. Because wasn't there always a juggernaut of a disaster heading your way?

The group slowly made their way through the

forest, their trek much slower due to all the stuff they were transporting. David became more and more impatient as time wore on, wanting to get this load home, because he felt a paranoia creeping up on him. Now would be a grand time for something to go wrong, right when they were transporting a load of precious cargo.

But as they walked on, eventually crossing the bridge and then heading up along the path and through the little intersection where he'd initially found Jim and his family, they didn't run into any real trouble. Beyond a few zombies and a pair of stalkers that tried to attack them, there was nothing.

They reached the campgrounds not much later.

As he walked in, David saw that the place was alive with activity. One of the newer people was on watch and he waved to them after he saw that it was the campground's leadership on approach, and they waved back. Some people were gathering firewood, some kids were running around, playing tag, some people were working on the fence, now adding on that secondary layer they'd talked about.

It gave him a powerfully good feeling, a warmth and a great comfort, coming home to this. As they made their way to the main office, he saw Amanda out and about. As soon as she saw him, she immediately blushed and looked away, then continued heading wherever it was she was going.

"Oh my," Cait said. "She *likes* you, David."

"Apparently," he muttered, thinking back to the previous night.

Damn, how the tables had turned. She'd been teasing him for weeks, flirting with him and hitting on him, giving him all these suggestive looks and smirks, operating from a position of clear power. Not anymore, apparently. He'd gained the power and he didn't even know how.

Well, that wasn't true. He imagined it had a lot to do with the fact that before she'd been merely entertaining the idea of sleeping with a cute young guy, and she had a sort of 'I can take you or leave you' attitude towards him. Not disrespectful per se, more that she kind of wanted him, not needed him.

Now though…

Now she knew how good he felt inside of her, and apparently it was *really* fucking good. He imagined she wanted him, and was embarrassed by how much she wanted him. He certainly knew that feeling, but how much more powerful must it be when you were used to being the one with all the power?

In his experience, attractive women got to pick and choose who they took to bed, and guys like him took what they could get. Although that had been less true recently, for some reason. David made himself focus as they brought the sledges out to the front of the main office, and Ashley and April came out to meet them.

"Wow! That's quite a haul, and you are...*so* fucking tall," Ashley said, staring up at Vanessa in something like wonder. "Hi."

"Hello," Vanessa replied with a smirk.

"This is Vanessa. She's from the doctor's group," David said.

"Awesome," Ashley replied.

April came over to him and he gave her a hug and a kiss. "Hi, love," he said.

She smiled broadly and looked down briefly. "Hi, love," she replied softly. "It looks like you found quite a lot."

"Yes! We finally can start repairing the cabins," David replied. "Do you think the two of you could organize this stuff and start work on the repairs? We'd stick around and help but we really have to get back to Jennifer, because we may be on the edge of another huge cache of supplies."

"Yeah, we've got this," Ashley replied. "You think you'll be back by tonight?"

"Almost certainly," Cait said.

"Can *you* come spend the night?" Ashley asked, staring up at Vanessa with what seemed to be an 'I think I'm in love' expression.

Vanessa just smirked. "Maybe."

"I would very much like that."

"I can tell. I'll see what I can do."

They finished checking in with Ashley and April, and after taking a short break, the four of them headed back out into the cold.

...

"Oh, wow, everyone's here," Jennifer said as she opened the door, though she sounded pleased instead of anxious.

"Yep, we decided to come to you," David replied.

"Good! Please, come in...hi, Vanessa."

"Hello, Jennifer," Vanessa said.

"We made a great haul at the construction site," David said as they all walked in.

"Awesome! I finished fixing the tool, it should be ready to go."

"Excellent news," Cait said, "but I'm sensing a 'but'."

"No but," Jennifer replied, though she looked

very bashful, "more of a, uh, request."

"What's that?" Cait asked, smiling in such a way that David had the idea that she already knew what the request was going to be.

"Will you...pleasure me? Like before?" she asked, her voice low, looking very embarrassed. Cait just smirked. Jennifer looked at the others. "I appreciate all you do for me, too!" she said quickly. "All three of you are really good, it's just, Cait...the things she can do..."

"It's okay, Jennifer," David said, "believe me, I know. Cait's amazing."

"Yes," Evie agreed immediately.

"Wow, you really must be something," Vanessa said, looking at Cait in a speculative and appraising kind of way.

"Yep," the redhead replied.

"We should hook up sometime soon."

"Yep," Cait repeated.

"In the meantime," Vanessa said, looking now at David, then at Evie, "I bet your boyfriend would absolutely *love* having a pair of goliaths taking turns riding him."

"Would you, David?" Evie asked.

"Obviously," he replied immediately, making them both laugh.

"So, sex break then?" Cait asked.

"Yes," David said, as Evie and Vanessa nodded.

"Okay. We can do it downstairs. I already took a bath, I think my bed should be enough to hold two of you at a time, so long as one of you is David," Jennifer said, eagerly taking Cait's hand and tugging her off towards the basement.

"Fun times," Cait murmured and let herself be taken.

David looked from Evie to Vanessa, who both looked down at him, and felt lust hit him in the gut like a hammer. He began to follow after the other two, and the goliath women followed him. Vanessa had to duck to get into the basement. As soon as they got close enough to the bed, Vanessa gave David a little push that sprawled him onto his back.

"Do you want to go first?" she asked, glancing at Evie.

She just smiled. "No," she replied, looking at him fondly, "you can go first. Just be gentle with him."

"I won't hurt him," Vanessa replied, setting aside her weapons and backpack. She looked down at him and he stared up at her. She looked absolutely enormous, towering over him in all her eight feet of inhuman glory. As she took off her shirt, he studied her huge, wonderful body. Her curious mixture of having pretty well-defined muscles in one place, and sexy, sexy padding and curves in others. Her pale blonde hair was pulled into a ponytail, and she revealed her huge thighs and broad hips as she took off her pants.

"Wow," he whispered.

"Yep. Now," she said, reaching down and undoing his pants with strong, sure fingers, "I'm a little impatient, and I think we're probably short on time, if we want to wrap this up before nightfall, so I'll just suck you off a little, then we go for a ride."

"Fine by me," he said.

She snorted. "Go figure."

She got his cock out, which was completely erect by now, and fully got down onto her knees before him. He heard Jennifer cry out and saw that she and Cait were on the floor now, among some bedding they'd pilled up for the occasion. Both of them were naked and marvelously beautiful, Cait's head now in between Jennifer's slim thighs.

She looked like an icon of sex on her hands and knees, pale and nude and glorious, her movements confident and sure as she began to eat out Jennifer, who herself looked marvelously sexual on her back, equally pale and nude and beautiful.

David wasn't religious or spiritual, but he found himself wanting to believe that there was something divine about watching one woman pleasure another.

"Oh my fucking...ahhhh..." David groaned as his attention was immediately and forcibly returned back to the woman before him. She was taking his cock into her big mouth, her wonderfully hot, wet, big mouth and her luscious lips and her skillful tongue. Vanessa chuckled softly as she took his whole dick easily into her mouth, closed her lips, and started sucking and bobbing her head. She kept at it for barely half a minute, coating his cock in a healthy layer of her saliva, before taking it back out and making shooing motions.

"Back," she said.

He nodded and pushed himself back onto the bed until his head hit the pillow. She climbed onto the bed and atop him, and the bed groaned under her weight, but held. He stared up at her in awe. He'd never been ridden by someone this much larger than him. She was the biggest woman he'd ever slept with, eight fucking feet tall and not thin, either, but built and pleasant thick in some areas. She looked like some kind of warrior goddess as she settled over him, her enormous breasts, easily the biggest he'd ever seen, swayed with each movement.

"I'm learning that goliaths like to be on top," David murmured as she finished getting into position above him.

"It's my favorite position and no one ever lets me do it," she replied, reaching down and gripping his cock. "But you will."

"Yes, he will," Evie said. "He trusts us."

"Like I said, I won't hurt you. I just want...oh yeah..." she whispered as she got him inside of her. She lowered herself, her thighs bulging, and she reached out and placed her hands on the wall above the bed, taking him all the way into her.

"Holy fucking shit," he groaned, reaching out, his hands finding her immense hips. "You are...*so* fucking huge, Vanessa," he whispered.

"Yes, I am," she replied with a grin and she began to fuck him.

He listened to Jennifer moan and cry out in pleasure as he started to groan himself. Her vagina was slippery, wet perfection, pure, hot paradise. He felt the bed shake beneath him as she rode him, slowly picking up speed, her movements careful. And just fucking...the pleasure! The raw, perfect pleasure of having Vanessa's bare pussy taking his cock again and again.

It burned him up, ate him alive, slid slowly through his body, radiating out from his cock, filling him. He grabbed her enormously broad hips, enjoying the unreal feeling of having an eight foot woman riding him, but soon became too enamored by her just impossibly huge tits hanging over his head. He reached up and began groping them.

Vanessa laughed softly. "I knew you couldn't resist."

"Could anyone?" Evie asked.

Vanessa gasped softly as he hit something sensitive inside of her, then closed her eyes and began to ride him more vigorously, though still keeping careful not to hurt him. He watched his cock disappearing into her wonderful goliath vagina again and again as he groped her ungodly huge tits. She rode him for another moment longer, then let out a soft sigh.

"I guess I'm hogging him, huh?" she asked.

"A little," Evie said with a smirk.

"Sorry."

"Oh I totally get it, I do the same thing. It's hard sharing him sometimes," Evie replied.

"I bet."

"Not that he minds," Evie said as Vanessa got up and she mounted him. "*You* tend to win out regardless. You're pretty cool as long as you're getting fucked."

"And you aren't?" he replied as she began to slide him into her pussy.

"Of course I am," she murmured. "And now that I have you and Cait and April in my life, I get fucked almost as much as I want to."

"Oh, almost, huh?"

"Yes-ah! Right there!" she moaned and began riding him, making the bed creak and groan again.

"I guess I'll have to step it up, huh?" he groaned, now grabbing her broad, pale hips.

"I think you're doing fine," she whispered, panting. "Ooh that's good. I love your cock."

"Oh, *Cait!*" Jennifer screamed and from the sounds she began to make he knew Cait had gotten her to orgasm. Either he was losing track of time or she really *was* that much better at getting a climax out of Jennifer, because that was *tough*.

He still remembered the black eye she'd given him when he'd given her that orgasm the first time they'd met.

"As soon as we get done with this little spree of ours," Evie panted, her huge, pale breasts swaying beautifully over his head, "you and I are going to have like, a whole day of sex."

"Can I come?" Cait asked.

"We all can come," Evie replied. "Speaking of which...don't move, David..."

She began to go faster, grinding his cock around inside of her for a bit, then moving rapidly up and down, her huge tits bouncing, her voice going up in pitch as she cried out, building towards her own beautiful climax and then…

"OH FUCK, DAVID!" she screamed and he felt her start to come.

He groaned, digging in his fingertips as he gripped her hips more tightly, and felt her come and it was so hot and so wet and so fucking good on his cock. He somehow barely managed to hold onto his own orgasm, because Vanessa was going to want another turn and he had to admit that, right now, he *really* wanted to come inside of her.

There was something especially, exceptionally satisfying about shooting his load into that eight foot goliath's bare pussy. He stared up at Evie, at one of the women he loved, as she came, lost in her orgasm but somehow still present enough to keep from hurting him, thankfully.

Goliaths, in his experience, had a lot of self-control.

She finished coming on him, making quite a wet spot on his shirt and pants and boxers, (this was exactly why he kept a spare change of clothes with him), and then she was left panting, planting her hands on either side of his head, staring at him.

Finally, she leaned down and kissed him. "I love you so much, David," she said as she pulled back.

"I love you too, Evie," he replied.

"You two make a cute couple," Vanessa said, then glanced at Cait, "a good trio."

"With April we make a great quad," Cait replied, then gasped.

David glanced down. They had switched places. Now Jennifer was pleasuring Cait's pussy with her tongue and fingers.

Evie climbed off of him and within five seconds Vanessa had reasserted herself, slipping him back inside of her. "My turn."

"I'm going to be fucking soaked," he muttered.

"Yes, you are," she agreed, then she began to ride him again.

There was that burning hot pleasure once more, eating a slow burn into him, melting him, consuming him. He immediately reached up and began groping her absurdly large breasts, drawn to them, and he held onto them as she fucked him faster and faster, the bed shaking and groaning beneath them.

It didn't take Vanessa much longer to reach her own climax, and having her come while on top of him was truly an experience. The huge goliath gripped the frame of the bed tightly as she began to orgasm, a loud, crying moan torn from her lips as her muscles tensed and went rigid, and she began to shake as it rolled through.

And he felt the immediate effects of it as she began to squirt, as she got hotter inside, as her vaginal muscles trembled around his rigid length. And as she began to ride him faster as she came, he was thrown headlong into his own orgasm and it was amazingly glorious. He groaned, hips thrusting up and forcing his cock deeper into her as the first volley of his seed was released, and she cried out.

Both of them moaned in a rapturous union and he reached out for her and she immediately took his hands in hers, lacing their fingers, her hands so much bigger than his. They held hands as they came together, and she stared down at him with wide, lust laced eyes, and he could feel his seed leaving him, spurting out of him as waves upon waves upon waves of pleasure exploded from his core with resounding explosions of sexual rapture.

When the orgasms left them, they both stayed like that for a long moment, then slowly released each other.

"Whew, I felt that one," Cait said.

"Yeah, our boyfriend really seems to agree with you," Evie murmured.

"Evidently," Vanessa replied, her eyes wide as she got her breath back. Finally, she let go of him and got up. She tracked down some water and began to wash herself up.

"You okay, love?" Cait asked, sitting down next to him.

"I'm great," he managed. "Uh...we need to get back to work, don't we?"

"Sadly, yes," Cait replied. She patted his thigh. "Get up, lover boy, and wash off."

He nodded and, after a few seconds, got up.

CHAPTER TEN

David could feel excitement coursing through him, and as they made their final approach to the bunker, he could tell that it wasn't just him.

Even Jennifer seemed to have a spring in her step. They were all anxious to get the bunker open. It had been there for decades, longer than any of them had been alive, apparently locked up, totally sealed.

Were there people inside? Were they alive? Dead?

From what he'd gathered about the idea of these bunkers, if this actually was a bunker as he understood it, was that people built them to be impenetrable, and then filled them with decades worth of food, water, power, medicine, everything they would need to survive.

Even if it worked...to what end? Was it worth living in one structure for decades with no access, literally, to the outside world?

Maybe it was to some people.

Well, if there were people down there, they were sure as fuck in for an unpleasant surprise.

Probably the strangest fact of life before the apocalypse, to David at least, was the notion that inhumans did not exist. At all. Not even a little. That was crazy. How much of a shock would it be to emerge from that world into this new one where eight foot people and lizard people and half-undeads existed alongside humans?

Either way, they were getting inside.

If there were people inside, he was more than willing to just leave them alone, if that's what they wanted, but he really hoped not. It would be sad, in a way, that someone had gone to all this trouble to set something like this up and never make it, but...honestly, it'd be better for him and his group. They stepped into the clearing with the bunker.

The only way to find out was to do it.

Some of their jubilance faded away as they again caught sight of the field of unmoving lumps among the snow. The dozens and dozens of dead stalkers, frozen for now. Eventually spring would come and they would thaw and rot and then another winter would come and refreeze them, and then it'd repeat until there was nothing left. But, thankfully, there didn't seem to be anymore in the area. He hoped that would keep.

After the factory, David had had enough with the undead for the day. For the week.

Shit, for the rest of his life, honestly.

Not that it mattered.

They made it to the bunker. "Okay, how much time do you need?" Cait asked.

"A few minutes, I think," Jennifer replied as she pulled out her device.

She crouched in front of the entrance and got to work. David kept his pistol out as he began to make a slow circuit along the outside of the bunker, warily eyeing the dead forest that surrounded them. Still nothing moved out there, but he'd learned to never drop his guard if he could afford it. His walk brought him back around to the starting point and revealed nothing new. So he stood there with Evie, Cait, and Vanessa while Jennifer worked her magic.

"I have to say, I'm really impressed with all of you," Vanessa said.

"Really?" Cait asked.

"Yes. Do you have *any* idea how many people

I've come across in my time? Hundreds. Over a thousand, probably. I spent a lot of time traveling. It's rare for people to actually *do* shit, you know? Most people are content to work simple jobs and live simple lives, and honestly, I fucking get that. I do. Doing shit is fucking hard. I mean, that's where I'm at now. I run security for a group of doctors. Sometimes I explore. Mostly I just relax nowadays. But even among the people who go out and do shit, I mean a lot of them fail. But here you all are, making shit happen. And not just any shit, you're *helping people.* I mean, even among the people who go out and successfully make shit happen, mostly it's just for themselves. This is rare. And I'm impressed. I'm happy to be a part of it, honestly. I like what you stand for," she explained.

"Well...thanks," David replied.

"Vanessa..." Evie said, her tone becoming mildly cautious, making Vanessa look at her curiously, "do you think there could be a chance of your group ever joining our group?"

Vanessa continued looking at her. David glanced at Evie, as did Cait. It was a good question, one he *had* considered.

"I don't know," she admitted finally. "If it were my decision, I'd say yes. I think Katya would agree with me. But we're not in charge. Donald is the one in charge, and he is...a very nervous, paranoid man. He likes you all, and you're gaining his trust, but he's had it rough. They all have. I think they're very attached to their notion of independence. But that might not remain feasible, not forever, maybe not even in the short term. We've had a lot of stalker attacks."

"Where would we even put them?" Cait

murmured.

"I don't know," Evelyn admitted. "Even if we fixed up all the cabins, I'm not sure we'd have room." She sighed softly. "It's just an idle question right now. I guess we shouldn't get too far ahead of ourselves."

"Well, it *is* a good idea to be thinking about the future," David said. "But yes, I guess it would be a bridge to cross later."

"I've got it!" Jennifer said, derailing the conversation.

Everyone looked at her and tightened their grips on their weapons. "We should probably get into some kind of position," David said.

They all agreed and Cait joined him in covering the door. Evie and Vanessa decided to stay out of sight for the moment, sticking to the walls on either side of the entryway. After instructing them on how to open it, Jennifer did the same.

David moved over to the locking mechanism and looked at Cait. She was crouched and off-center, weapon aimed at the door. She gave him a tight nod. David, pistol in one hand, used the other to initiate the opening procedure. There was a cracking sound and then a pair of loud clicks, and then the door went inwards a few inches.

They waited. Nothing happened.

He found that it was basically just a fancy, heavy metal door on hinges and pushed it inward. It swung slowly in, creaking as it did, and pointed his flashlight in while carefully leaning around the corner, exposing as little of himself as he could. A dark, metal stairway, descending into the earth, sat on the other side.

There was nothing and nobody inside of it. He

pointed his light down it and saw that it ended maybe fifteen feet down, in another metal door.

It all looked like it hadn't been touched in years.

"Okay, clear," he said. "Jennifer, with me, everyone else, wait here."

They didn't argue with him, at least. David led the way with his pistol and his flashlight. The metal stairs were extremely solid and unmoving under his feet. This place felt practically new, though everything was covered in a fine layer of dust. Maybe untouched was a better word.

They reached the bottom without incident, and it was dead silent save for the soft whispering of the wind from up above. The sun shone coldly down into the stairway, and he saw lightbulbs built into the ceiling that were dead. There was a simple switch on the wall next to the door.

He reached out and flipped it. Nothing happened. No power, apparently. Well, the solar panels had been taken from the place.

"Okay, Jennifer, can you open this next one?" he asked.

"Hold on." She crouched in front of another locking mechanism built into the door and studied it for a few seconds. "Yeah, actually. This one will be easier."

She set to work. He listened to her picking the lock and watched her work. Her movements had an inhuman precision to them, and he wondered if it was because of the fact that she was a wraith. Everything she did was perfect and precise. He wondered, suddenly, if that's why she was as good a shot as she was, even though she said she wasn't much of a fighter. His thoughts were again derailed as she suddenly stood up.

"Okay, it's ready to be opened."

"All right, head back up and send Cait down."

"Okay...stay safe," she said, and kissed him, then jogged back up the stairs. A moment later, Cait joined him.

"We ready?" she asked.

"Yeah," he replied, then looked around unhappily. There *was* a very small room at the bottom of the stairs, but there was hardly any place to be without directly being in front of the door. If someone was behind it with a gun, it would be a *real* gamble.

"I'm ready, honey," Cait said, crouching on the stairs against the left wall with her pistol aimed at the doorway.

"Okay, here we go," he replied.

David slipped to the right and initiated the open button. The door opened and went in a few inches. He pushed on it and waited for something to happen.

"It looks clear. It's dark," Cait said softly.

"I'm going in," David replied.

He peered cautiously around the door frame and saw that she was right. The light from the sun up above and their flashlights showed what looked to be a decent-sized square room. He expected to see something made of metal or perhaps concrete, but that wasn't the case at all. It almost looked like the kind of room you'd find in a house.

Actually, that's exactly what it looked like. There was wallpaper and carpeting, as well as a few end tables and even a couch against the back wall directly across from him, in between a pair of doors that looked much closer to regular doors. Everything felt completely still, totally silent, totally dead.

He very seriously doubted anyone was in here, but they had to be sure.

"Go tell the others we're okay," David said, "and that it looks empty, and have Evie come down here. We'll search it."

"Okay," Cait said, and jogged back up the stairs.

He stepped in through the doorway and quickly looked around, but the place still seemed empty, almost like they had cracked open a tomb that hadn't seen the light of day in a century. He saw six doors, two ahead, two to the left, two to the right, all closed, all of them the kind of doors you'd find in an above ground house. A moment later, Cait and Evie, ducking a bit, returned. She straightened up as she stepped into the room.

"Well, this is...not what I expected. It's what I hoped for, though," she murmured.

"We need to clear it," David said.

"Okay then, room by room," Cait replied, and they got to it.

The next fifteen minutes were spent carefully inspecting each door and whatever lay beyond. The first was a lavish bedroom with a king size bed and very comfortable looking pillows and bedding, a pair of dressers, a big cabinet that held a flat television and a few curious electronic devices, slim black boxes with buttons and small screens, were tucked away in some shelves beneath it.

After a moment, he realized he was looking at media players, movie players, though he couldn't for the life of him remember what they were supposed to be called. Something with letters strung together in an otherwise meaningless fashion.

He ignored them and moved on. There were two other doors in that room. One led to a large, walk-in closet packed with fancy-looking clothing and shoes, and more bedding, which would be decently useful.

The other was a huge bathroom that had a shower cubicle, a pair of toilets, two sinks, and a large tub. All of it looked untouched. They moved on, coming to the next room, which seemed to be a recreational area.

There were couches, a table, another television and more devices, a pool table, (those had survived the transition into the new world, he'd come across enough of them in motels and bars,) and another two doors at the back. One led to a closet that was packed with boxes, tons and tons of colorful cardboard boxes, what Cait identified as board games, which he *had* encountered before, though mostly people played cards now.

And the second door led to…

"Oh my God," David whispered. "April is going to be *so* happy."

"Holy shit, she's going to flip out," Cait agreed.

It was a little library. It was about twice the size of the closet, and was essentially a lounging couch in the center of the room, surrounded on all sides by bookshelves that were packed full. There had to be hundreds, maybe over a thousand books there.

They moved on, and every room after that revealed something fantastically useful.

The next was a dining room and kitchen combination, with a *huge* store of food at the back. There were dozens upon dozens of crates of cans and vacuum-sealed packages of all kinds of food, fruits and vegetables and meats and seasonings and tons of other things.

There was also a big, complicated looking, bulky machine in one corner that they realized was a water-filtration device. David knew that this room by itself meant that everything they had gone through to get here was absolutely, totally worth it.

And then they cracked open the rest of the place.

The next room was a generator room, and not only did it have a generator that ran off of bio-mass, but there were six spare solar panels tucked away, still in their packaging, and there was even a pair of exercise bikes that had been rigged to produce energy.

The next room revealed an infirmary that was packed with a tremendous amount of basic medical supplies, everything from bandages to antibiotics to painkillers to everyday medical tools, but also a lot of more complex items, what seemed to be surgical tools, and specialized medications, and more. Vanessa, who had eventually come down to join them, was particularly excited about this find.

The last room was the smallest, but contained items no less important.

It was an armory.

They found a half-dozen gun lockers that held pistols, shotguns, and rifles, automatic rifles and even a few sniper and hunting rifles, as well as hundreds upon hundreds of rounds of ammo and shells. They also found full sets of body armor, hunting knives, even some explosives.

"Holy fucking shit, I can't believe someone created all this and just...left it here," Vanessa whispered as she carefully picked through the arsenal.

"They probably died," Cait said.

"Probably. Good for us," Vanessa replied.

"And it's just been sitting here all this time," Jennifer said, a sense of wonder in her voice. "It's so hard to believe no one has ever been in here after they closed the door probably fifty years ago. It's just...it doesn't seem real."

"I know what you mean," David replied.

"Okay," Evie said, "we've got a massive amount of work ahead of us if we want to get this all home safely."

David nodded, knowing she was right. This was going to be a big project.

They got to work.

...

It took almost three days to finish their work.

They barely managed to get a big haul home before night set in that first day, and Vanessa had ended up spending the night. After that, it got tough, because stalker activity picked up in the area. After having some difficulty going back to the bunker, they'd finally convinced Donald to let Katya help in exchange for one of the exercise bikes, a solar panel, and some more of the rarer medications and medical tools.

They'd also brought Ashley, Richard, and Lena for extra protection and hauling power, and had spent all of the next day, and most of the day after that cleaning out the bunker. As soon as they did, David had Jennifer seal it back up.

After that, with a storm brewing on the horizon, they'd hustled to head back to the construction site and to get the rest of the materials there, then had hauled it back home. From there, David, Cait, and Evie had traveled back to the hospital with Vanessa and Katya and a care package of probably a third of the medical supplies they'd found in the bunker. There, they had cemented an alliance with the doctors as formally as they could.

In exchange for all the supplies they'd given

them, and an agreement to help them out if they needed it in the future, the doctors agreed to provide medical services to their settlement if they needed it, and Vanessa and Katya would help them do dangerous things if and when that came up.

And then they'd gone back home as the snow started to fall, and had just made it in for a large, fantastic dinner as a powerful snow storm settled in. Spirits were high and David had to admit that he was feeling better than he had in a long time.

It felt like they'd finally made actual, real progress. They had almost everything they had set out to get, and really, there was just one thing left on the item list. But that could wait for the time being, as David had other things on his mind. Now that dinner had died down, he thought it was time again to discuss more serious things.

He looked around at Cait and Evie and April and Jennifer and Ashley and Amanda. They had all decided to come join them for dinner in the main office, and he had the idea that Amanda intended to finally approach him again for more sex. He'd almost swear she'd been avoiding him for the past few days, but now, here she was.

That would come later, though.

"So...we've gotten almost everything we've needed," he began.

"Almost everything?" Jennifer asked. "I thought that was everything."

"We still need a hydroponic garden," David replied.

"Yes," Cait said, nodding. "One of the most crucial things I've learned is that you need everything you can to hedge against disaster. We have no idea when we might be faced with a drought, or shit, flooding, or an army of humans or undead, or a fire. The more avenues of resources we can create for ourselves, the better. Ideally, I want this place completely self-sufficient."

"I have to agree," Evie said.

"But where would we even find one? Or find the materials to build one?" April asked.

"Technically, we could rig one so long as we have good soil, sun lamps, seeds, a proper apparatus, power, and a few other things," Jennifer murmured.

"Cait?" he asked.

"For some reason, I remember the fishers talking about a hydroponic garden earlier this year, but I can't remember why or in what context. Otherwise..." she sighed and shook her head. "I have no idea where we might find the materials to build one."

"All right, we'll check with them. It dovetails nicely with the next part of the plan," David said.

"What *is* the next part?" Evie asked.

"I want to run something by all of you. We have found an abundance of resources over the past week. We shared some of it with the hospital crew. I want to share with the other groups in the region. The farmers, the fishers,...and Lima Company."

"Lima Company?" Cait asked uncertainly.

"Yes," David replied.

"I don't know," Evie murmured. "I mean, I'm down to share at least something with the other two. I think you're right, we need to build alliances and trust, but Lima Company hasn't traditionally been very, well, trustworthy."

"I know. Maybe it could be seen as a power move, though," David said.

"You really sure you want to pull a power move on Stern?" Cait asked uncertainly.

"Maybe I want to let him know that we aren't going to be fucked around with," David replied.

"That's...gutsy," Amanda said.

"I'm not interested in antagonizing or inviting violence, but hear me out. Word gets around. They're *going* to find out that we've had a big stroke of luck recently and have a big store of resources. We can't stop that. Given that is the case, I think since it is inevitable Lima Company is going to hear about that, they should hear about it directly from us," David said.

"That...actually makes a lot of sense," Amanda replied.

"Plus, I'm betting they won't actually take us up on any offer we give them. Stern's too proud. Also, we should touch base with Lara."

"You wanna touch more than her base," Cait said.

He chuckled and rubbed the back of his neck. "Can you blame me?"

"No. I want to touch her all over...is she into girls, did you find out?" she asked.

"I'm not sure," he replied.

"I fucking hope so, god*damn* that girl is so hot."

"Speaking of that, uh...if there's nothing else, David, Cait, could I talk to you? In private?" Amanda asked, garnering everyone's attention.

"Is there anything else?" David asked, feeling a stab of lust hit him right in the gut.

"No. We can figure out logistics tomorrow," Evie replied. She smiled broadly at them. "Go have fun, you three."

"Thank you," Amanda said, standing.

"I'm very eager to have this conversation," Cait said, getting up as well.

"Yep," David said. He followed the two women quickly upstairs and soon all three of them were standing in his and Evie's bedroom.

"Okay, Amanda, what's up?" Cait asked, sitting down in one of the chairs and staring at her intently. David stood beside Cait, also waiting.

She laughed, suddenly nervous. "Um, well, I guess I'll just dive in. I'm not used to being the one who's nervous in the bedroom. I've been pretty confident up until now."

"Why lose confidence?" Cait asked, sounding honestly curious.

"Well, for one, David is...*amazing* in bed. I wasn't ready for that. I mean, don't get me wrong, I didn't think you'd be bad or anything, I just didn't think you'd have...just the *best* dick I've found in years. And, the other reason is, well..." She laughed nervously. "Normally I'm all about guys. Almost all the time. But sometimes I've been known to go for chicks. I'd say one out of every hundred, maybe even five hundred, women that I see get me going. But when they do, they *really* do. And Cait, you are just, um, you are one of the most attractive women I've ever seen. And the fact that you and David are together, it makes the whole thing a lot hotter. So, what I'm saying is, I want to have a threesome with both of you, if that's okay."

Cait laughed softly. "Yes, Amanda, that sounds great. You're a very sexy woman."

"Obviously I'd love to," David replied.

"I figured. Okay then, so shall we?"

"We shall," Cait said, standing and taking off her shirt.

The three of them spent the next few minutes hastily stripping naked, washing up, and then crawling into his and Evie's huge bed together.

"This bed is *so* big," Amanda murmured.

"Yep. *So* much absolutely *filthy* fucking has happened in this bed," Cait replied. She grinned as she crawled on top of Amanda and planted her hands on either side of her head. She stared down at her. "Tell me if I'm going too fast."

"Okay," Amanda replied, staring back up at her.

David watched as his redheaded lover leaned down and pressed her lips to Amanda's. The mature, married woman responded immediately, like she'd been electrified, and began to passionately make out with her. Cait didn't miss a beat as Amanda began to run her hands over all her smooth, pale skin. The two women began to make out intensely, groping each other, moaning as they locked lips and twisted tongues.

They continued kissing for a long moment, and then Cait broke away and began to kiss across her face, down her neck, across her collarbone, and then across her breasts. Amanda was breathing heavily at this point, shivering each time Cait's luscious lips came in contact with her beautiful, pale skin.

"Oh my..." she whispered. "It's been a long time since I've been in a threesome, and it's been even longer since I've been in a threesome with another woman. Years, actually. And I think you might be the most attractive woman I've ever been intimate with."

"She's also the most skilled woman you've ever been intimate with," David said, getting closer. "You're going to lose your mind when she starts going down on you."

"I hope so," Amanda replied grinning, then she reached out, laid a hand across the back of his neck, and pulled him closer.

As Cait began sucking on her tits, on her beautiful pink nipples, he and Amanda started to make out. Her lips felt wonderfully hot against his, and her tongue darted skillfully into his mouth, dancing with his own. He tasted her and felt her moving against him, and Cait too, moving against them both as she lavished Amanda's sensitive breasts with attention and pleasure, licking across them, across her nipples, sucking on them, eliciting moans from her.

"You get to be the center of this threesome," David said in between kisses.

"Mmm-hmm," Cait agreed. "We've had a lot of them recently, so you can just lay back, relax, and get fucked happily."

"After everything I've gone through over the past several months, I really, really like the sound of that," Amanda replied.

Cait smiled and then slipped lower, until she was laying on her stomach in between Amanda's pale, spread-open legs. She leaned down, gently spread the taut lips of her pussy, and then got to work pleasuring her.

Amanda let out a loud, almost startled moan as Cait began putting her tongue to use. She started to writhe and shudder as the pleasure began to hit her, and she resumed making out with David with a renewed intensity. He kissed her back, groping her breasts as she shoved her tongue into his mouth, and felt her reach down. One hand went to the back of Cait's head, the other wrapped around his cock and began to massage it slowly.

He kissed her for another minute or so until it became too much for her and she stopped being able to focus on anything but what Cait was doing to her.

She moaned and panted and cried out, clearly trying to control herself as she shook and shuddered, and now she was grasping the blanket beneath her, her pale legs spread open wide. David slipped lower and began to suck on one of her breasts, and she cried out again.

"Oh my fucking-oh! You two are...oh too much...too much..." she panted.

Neither of them relented. They both continued pleasuring her, going and going until she had to clap her hands over her mouth as an orgasm suddenly began to consume her. David watched as she screamed behind her hands, her hips bucking furiously as she began to come, and Cait kept fingering her, fucking her with two of her fingers all through the orgasm, making her shake and scream even more powerfully.

When she was finished some time later, she collapsed against the bed, panting, gasping really. "Now...now I know what they mean," she whispered.

"They?" Cait asked.

"Your girlfriends, and Jennifer, they all told me...oh my...told me how good you are at oral. Fuck," she whispered, then she took a deep breath and let it out slowly. She looked at David suddenly. "Will you fuck me? I have *really* been wanting you to fuck me again."

"Yeah," he replied, and Cait laughed and made room.

"He's pretty great, huh?" she asked.

"My God, yes," Amanda replied. "I'm not sure what it is, honestly."

"Sometimes, a vagina is just the right size and shape for a particular dick," Cait replied with a shrug. "That's just the way biology falls occasionally."

"I'm so glad it fell this way," Amanda said as David got on top of her.

"Me too," he agreed.

She grabbed his cock before he could properly get into position and pulled him closer. Well, she wasn't fucking around, apparently. As soon as she got him lined up with her exceptionally wet pussy, he pushed his way inside. She opened her legs wide, folding them, and moaned loudly, so loudly, as he penetrated her.

"Wow, you *do* love his cock," Cait murmured.

"Yes...yes! I do!" she cried as he started fucking her.

"Ah, fuck, Amanda," he groaned as he slid smoothly in and out of her.

Her pussy was *so* fucking wet right now. He got all the way into her, that hot, hot ecstasy filling him, and she reached up, grabbing him and pulling him against her. They kissed passionately as he made love to her, beginning to hammer away at that sweet, married MILF pussy. He had to admit, he was fucking loving the reaction he was getting out of her.

This must be what Ellie felt like when he fucked her. There was something so powerful, so wonderful about screwing someone who was obviously getting a fucking shitload of pleasure out of what you were doing to them.

Cait laid down beside them, watching them intently as they screwed like rutting animals, her eyes filled with lust. As they continued fucking, Amanda slowly began to unfold her legs, putting her feet up in the air, and she grabbed at his back, shoving her tongue into his mouth, moaning into the kissing with a powerful intensity.

"I'm coming!" she screamed suddenly, breaking

the kiss.

David groaned as he felt her pussy start to constrict and flutter, and she began to squirt and scream as he kept screwing her brains out.

She tried to keep in control but clearly couldn't, so Cait helped her, holding a hand tightly over her mouth.

"Wow, that must feel *so* fucking good," she murmured.

"It does..." David groaned as he felt her squirting all over his dick and balls, felt that incredible, wet heat bathing him in bliss.

He fucked her throughout the orgasm and when she was finished, she went slack and Cait raised her hand. Amanda was panting, gasping, almost delirious with pleasure.

"Do me doggystyle," she panted.

"Okay," he replied, pulling out.

She took a few more seconds to get her breath back, then rolled over and got up onto her hands and knees, showing him her ass. She had a nice one, it was trim and fit, with just a bit of padding to it. He got up against her and slipped his cock back inside of her, grabbed her hips, and started hammering away at that sweet, married pussy again.

"Oh *fucking shit!*" she cried. "That's just...*so* good!"

"Yes, it is," he groaned in agreement. Her pussy felt so nice wrapped tight around his cock, that ultimate pleasure of raw vagina rubbing against your bare dick. He looked at Cait. "Get over here, you little slut."

"Yes, sir," she replied, getting closer.

He pulled his cock out for a moment and stuck it in her mouth. She started sucking him off, bobbing her head smoothly, and Amanda twisted back around to look at them. "Oh wow, that's so fucking hot," she whispered.

David let Cait suck him off for a bit longer, then pulled out and got back to smashing Amanda's pussy, making her cry out again.

"Cait!" she moaned. "If you...oh *fuck!* If you get in front of me, I'll eat you."

"Okay," Cait replied immediately, and got in front of Amanda, laying on her back and opening her legs.

"It's been a while since I've eaten pussy," she panted.

"You'll do fine," Cait replied.

Amanda buried her head in between Cait's thick, pale thighs as David kept ramming her from the back and her moans became muffled. Cait's own moans quickly joined hers as Amanda got to work. After all the hard work he'd been doing over the past week, especially today, this was a hell of a way to unwind.

"Harder!" Amanda begged as she kept pleasuring Cait.

"You got it," David replied. He slapped her tight ass and then grabbed her hips firmly and started pounding her brains out.

"Show her no mercy, David," Cait growled as she grabbed Amanda's head.

Their married fuck friend began moaning and crying out with a renewed intensity, still muffled as her face was buried completely in Cait's crotch. She was being used from both ends, and she seemed to absolutely love it. Within another minute or so, he had her coming again, delivering her third orgasm for the session, and this time he didn't hold back. He started coming along with her and quickly started draining his cock into her as she screamed and squirted once again.

He groaned, hunching over her, hips jerking automatically each time his cock released a fresh spray of his seed. His orgasm blossomed inside of him and spread to all the parts of his body, an amazing warmth of total bliss and sexual gratification that seemed to stretch on into forever.

And at some point it wore off, and he'd drained himself totally into her pussy, and he pulled out of her and sat down.

She moaned, falling forward onto Cait.

None of them spoke for a moment. Then he looked at Cait and she smiled at him and beckoned him closer.

It was her turn.

David began to move.

...

"David! Cait!"

"Hello, William," David replied.

The older man came to a stop at the edge of his farmland, his domain really, and shook their hands in turn. He seemed...happier. David remembered that the last time he'd been here, asking for help against the thieves, he had been harried and anxious. Whatever problem he was facing seemed to have passed and turned out for the best. He wished the farmers weren't so secretive, but honestly he couldn't blame them.

"So how is everything? The last time we spoke, uh..." he frowned suddenly as he probably remembered that he'd refused to help them.

"Everything went fine," David replied.

"Oh, uh, good. I'm sorry again we couldn't offer

any help..."

"It's fine," Cait said, and David nodded.

"It turned out okay. In fact, it all turned out very okay. The reason I'm here is because we've grown a bit, in terms of people and resources. And in the hopes of securing a more solid alliance, and just generally being good neighbors, I wanted to know if there was anything we could give to you from our stocks," he said.

"Really?" William asked, then seemed to consider it. "What's on offer?"

"Guns, bullets, medicine, mostly. Possibly some construction materials, but we're still sorting that out for ourselves right now, so I'm not sure what I can promise."

William stared at the two of them for a long moment, as if measuring them, then finally nodded. "Well, so far you two have proven quite trustworthy, and I can't really see a downside in cementing a more solid alliance, and being good neighbors. We could use medicine, specifically some antibiotics, but a general care package of the basic stuff would also be appreciated, as well as some nine millimeter bullets, and, if you've got them, some thirty aught six bullets as well."

"I'm positive we can swing that," David replied. "Is there anything else that needs doing? Any special jobs that you'd rather have someone else do?"

"Not at the moment, no, but that offer is very much appreciated and I'll keep you in mind." He sighed. "I'm getting more risk-averse in my old age..."

"I think that may just be a reaction to the times," David said. "I'm still young and *I've* certainly gotten a lot more risk-averse recently."

William chuckled a little grimly. "That's a fair point."

"Well, if there's nothing else, we'll send one of our people back with a care package."

"That sounds great. Thank you again."

"You're welcome."

They shook hands once more and then they began walking away. As they made their way through the forest, which was covered in a fresh layer of snow, David thought back to the last night, which had been exceptionally pleasant. The threesome had continued for almost another hour, with several breaks in between extended fuck sessions. He'd come something like five times, in and on both of the women, and that had been just...

Beyond amazing.

It had ended, eventually, and Amanda, (after a thorough washing), had gone home to her husband. And David didn't remember anything after that, because he'd been fucking exhausted, and had passed out almost as soon as she was gone. He remembered Evie riding him in the middle of the night, and then Ashley fucking him in the morning, practically demanding it.

After a wash and breakfast, Evie, April, Ashley, and even Jennifer, who was still hanging around, had gone to help the people that now made up their village. Though mostly Jennifer settled in to get to work on repairing or disassembling their mountain of guns.

He and Cait had decided to make their round trip. They'd already checked up on the hospital group once more, and everything was great over there. Apparently the farmers were good, and next on the list was Lima Company.

Cait had wanted to leave them for last, but David wanted to get them out of the way. Plus, he had to admit, he wanted to check up on Lara. He'd been a little worried about her, because the way Ellie had painted it, she had actually been risking her life going against Stern's orders. Would he *actually* kill her for that?

David didn't think so, but he also got the feeling that Stern was a man capable of a great many things, not all of them good.

And so they swung back by the village, updated them on the situation, and had Ashley take the care package out, as she was desperate to get back out into the world again. And once that was out of the way, they began making their way back towards the military outpost. As they walked through the woods, neither of them spoke, and David was reminded of how nice it was to be with someone where the silence was comfortable.

There were so many people he didn't talk with that he'd traveled with simply because he wasn't sure what to say, and it felt awkward or uncomfortable. It felt like they didn't need to speak with Cait, and Evie, and April, they were comfortable with each other and could just be in each other's presence, and that was enough.

They didn't talk until they reached the road that ran alongside the lake.

"So, I've thought some more about Jennifer and where she might live," Cait said.

"Oh yeah?"

"Yes. The basement of the main office. It's a decent size, big enough for someone to make a nice little place for themselves if we cleared it out, and I think she would like it. She seems most comfortable in her basement, although that could just be me projecting, or the fact that the only times I've seen her down there are when she's getting fucked," Cait replied.

"I think it makes sense," David said. "At the very least, we'll have a few options to present to her. The basement or that spare storage room...are you still comfortable in your own room?"

"Yeah, I like it. Although I could see giving it up. I'd be happy to share that big room with you and Evie, if you'd be comfortable with it. I spend most nights in there anyway."

"I'd be okay with it, I'm almost sure Evie would," David replied.

"I may just do that when I get farther along," she murmured, glancing down and laying a hand across her stomach, over her leather jacket.

"How are you doing...on that front, uh, so far?" he asked.

She laughed. "If it wasn't for my missed period, I still wouldn't even suspect. I feel like I always do. But I imagine that's going to change." She paused, then reached out and took his hand. "Thank you...for standing by me. I know this is scary, and unexpected, but I can't really tell you how much I appreciate that you're going to be involved."

"I want to be. I love you," he replied, lacing their fingers.

They walked along like that, descending into companionable silence once again, until they made their final approach to the military outpost. It looked just the same, and there was even a familiar figure standing atop the watchtower.

"David! Cait!" Lara said happily as they approached.

David felt relief hit him as he looked up at her. She looked good, and she seemed happy to see them. "Hello, Lara," Cait replied.

"How are you doing?" David asked.

"I'm good. Been busy. Stern was...less than happy that I left, and didn't really buy what I told him, so he's been working me hard. But it was still worth it," she replied. "How's everyone? How's it all going?"

"We found two new groups of people, they're living with us, and we found a big cache of supplies," David replied.

"Wow, really?! That's a lot of change, damn," she replied.

"Yep...could you get Stern? We're here to offer support in the form of supplies."

She frowned. "I doubt he'd say yes..."

"I doubt it, too. But...well, trust me, we've thought this through, and this is the thing we want to do," David replied.

"Okay, that's fair. I have to admit, I'm interested to see his response. Hold on." She turned around and called down to someone, then instructed them to go get Stern. While they waited, she turned back. "So...any other developments?"

"David and I had a very, very long night of *great* sex with a married woman last night," Cait replied with a smirk.

"Oh." Lara blushed and cleared her throat. "my. That's...interesting."

Cait laughed. "For a military woman, you're rather shy about sex."

"It's...complicated," she replied after a moment.

"It doesn't have to be. I assume you intend to pay David another visit at some point?"

Her blush deepened. "Yes," she replied quietly. "I fully intend to. When I get the chance. That may be a while, unfortunately..." She glanced back and then straightened up. A moment later, Stern climbed the watchtower and looked down at them.

"David. Cait. I understand you want my attention?" he asked, sounding vaguely amused.

"Yes," David replied. "We've recently happened into some luck. We have a good-sized reserve of supplies, and we're offering gifts to everyone in the region."

Stern raised an eyebrow. "Where did you find these...supplies?"

"You know, here and there," David replied.

"Hmm. Quite." He frowned slightly. "What, exactly, are you offering?"

"Food. Medical supplies. Weapons. Ammo. Some tools," he replied.

"I see," he replied, a little curtly. "Well, although I congratulate you on your find, and your neighborly attitude, I must state that we are quite fine in all departments. Now, if there is nothing else, I'm afraid I'm a busy man."

"No, nothing else," David replied.

"Then goodbye."

He turned and walked away. Lara watched him go, then turned back to them when he was gone. "So, that was interesting."

"Yeah. That's about what I'd hoped for, actually," David replied. He sighed. "I wish we could stick around and talk but we've got more to do."

"I understand. I promise, I'll come visit when I can, but I want to stress that it might be weeks," Lara replied.

"That's fine. We'll be there. It was good seeing

you, Lara," Cait said.

"You too!"

They said their farewells and then began walking to the fishing village.

CHAPTER ELEVEN

David half-expected to see something bad happening as they closed in on the fishing village.

The last time they'd been here, it had been in pretty poor condition. But not only was it bustling and busy, in what appeared to be a good way, so was the little collection of cabins they'd passed along the way. They'd had to help clear them out of vipers. David still had nightmares about the gray, dark-eyed horrors, creeping up out of the water at him in waves, coming to eat the flesh from his bones. They were their own special kind of disturbing.

Of course, weren't all the different types of undead?

As they approached slowly and visibly down the main path that led into the village, one of the group broke away. David recognized the village leader, Murray. There was something off-putting about the man, something that brought up distrust in David, but having reflected on it more, he thought that maybe it was just the way the man was, maybe he couldn't help but look like he was planning on screwing you over.

Of course, that didn't mean he wasn't planning to fuck you over.

But so far, their interactions had been positive at least.

"Hello," he said. "Been a little bit since I've seen you two. How are things?"

"Quite good. We come bearing gifts," David replied.

"Oh yeah? What kinda gifts?"

"Well, I guess more accurately, we *will* come

bearing gifts, once we know which gift you would like. We lucked into some supplies, and we're spreading the wealth around in the spirit of neighborly goodness," Cait said. "What do you need?"

"Oh, wow. That's a pleasant surprise. Mostly people come to us needing things, not offering. Or at least offering to trade. Do you actually plan on just giving us stuff?"

"Yes. I will say that we *are* hoping to cement a somewhat stable alliance. You help us, we help you kind of alliance, whenever something might arise."

Murray sighed and glanced back at the others as he scratched his chin, then looked back to him and Cait. "Okay, that's fair. You lot have proven pretty reliable so far. So yeah, I accept. As for what we could use: ammo. That's really it. And we've got a wide enough array of guns that any kind of ammo would be appreciated. Although I would specifically like some forty-fives, if you can spare it," he said to them.

"We can do that," David replied. "We'll get you a shipment of ammo soon. But before we do that, we have another, separate question."

"All right, I'm listening."

"We're looking for a hydroponic garden, or the materials to make one," Cait said. "For some reason, I seem to remember you or someone here mentioning that at some point over the past six months or so. Can you recall that?"

"Oh yes," he replied immediately. "There was a hydroponic garden, or what was left of one, over on the island." He turned and pointed. In the distance, maybe a few hundred meters away, near the center of the lake, was a decent-sized island. "We went over there during the summer to try and find some resources. There's stuff over there but it was way too dangerous. Lost a few people to the vipers over there. Haven't been back since."

"Well, shit. I don't suppose you'd be willing to lend us some boats? Possibly some backup? We really could use that garden," David murmured.

"Well..." he looked reluctant, but at the same time, he looked like he was going to say yes. David wasn't sure why, he just had that feeling. Finally, he sighed. "Maybe we can work something out. There's supplies on that island, but also something I need." He thought about it a bit longer and they waited. Finally, he nodded. "Okay. I'll send Ruby and my second in command, Gordon, over with you. I imagine you'll want to gather more people. Right now, we've only got three boats, not very big ones. They've got engines, though. Three people can fit in a boat, no more."

"How about a goliath?" David asked.

"I'd say they'd have to be by themselves," Murray replied.

"All right. We'll be back as soon as we can with the supplies and our people. Get the boats ready...what is it you need us to get over there?" Cait asked.

"I was one of the people over there during the summer. In all the chaos, I lost my lighter. Normally I'd let it go, but...it was my father's. I'd prefer that you make a serious effort to retrieve it while you're over there. I'll provide you with a map of where things are," he said.

"We'll make a serious effort," David promised.

"Thanks. I'll be here, getting everything ready."

They turned and hurried off.

...

In the end, it took two hours to get everything ready.

They returned to their campgrounds to meet with their inner circle and also gather up the ammunition care package. After explaining the plan, they'd debated for a while as to who should go. They decided that Vanessa should be on the expedition, which meant Evie wouldn't be. They also were going to ask Katya to come with them, because she probably had the most combat experience of them all.

Which meant that there would be just one seat left. They went back and forth a bit before ultimately deciding Jennifer should come with them, in case her technical expertise was needed for any reason. Ashley was, naturally, pissed for being left behind again, but thankfully was willing to stay behind without too much argument.

After catching lunch during the debate, he, Cait, and Jennifer geared up, grabbing a bit more of an arsenal than they were used to carrying around, and made the trek to the hospital. Given everything they'd done for them recently, Vanessa and Katya were eager to join them, and the others reluctantly allowed them to go. And so they'd geared up and then the group of now five made their way back to the fishing village. As they came back down the path, David felt a potent mixture of fear, anxiety, and excitement.

This was, as far as he knew, the last thing they had to deal with.

Not forever, but probably for the near future at least. After this, it would be just hanging around the campgrounds, getting shit done. He was really, really looking forward to that. Long days of simple work, good food, great times, and amazing sex.

He just had to survive this next part.

They all did.

"Over here!" Murray called.

David looked around and saw him farther down, at the head of a wooden dock that extended a little ways past the ice that had gathered at the edges of the lake. He saw two figures standing at the end of the dock, preparing the boats. He recognized one of them.

Ruby. He hesitated. She'd been shot, too. He didn't remember her wounds being terrible, but getting shot wasn't anything to shrug at. She looked good, though, her movements competent and sure and swift as she checked over the boats.

"So this is the team?" he asked, looking uncertainly at Vanessa.

"Yep," David replied. "And here is your care package." He passed the duffel-bag he'd been carrying over to him.

Murray accepted it, hefted it a few times, then nodded. "Thank you very much, sir. Here." He reached into his back pocket and passed David a piece of paper that had a simple sketch on it. "Pretty simple and straightforward. As you can see, there's a path that breaks off into three other paths. Left is where my lighter should be, right is the hydroponic garden, and forward was a building that we were going to check for supplies. So, if you can manage that, then that'd be beneficial, potentially, for both of us."

"All right," David replied, studying it for a bit, then passing it around to the others. "We'll be back as soon as we can. Are the boats ready?"

"Yeah, just about. I'll leave you to it. Good

luck," he said, and headed over to the main building of the village.

They walked down the dock to join Ruby and the other person, the man named Gordon. He was a wiry, stern-faced man with a head of dark hair and skin that looked heavily weathered and grizzled. He turned and looked at Vanessa, frowning. "I take it you're a hell of a fighter?" he asked.

"Why do you say that?" Vanessa replied.

"Because if you weren't, they wouldn't be trying to fit you onto one of these," he said, indicating the boats. One of them, at least, was a bit bigger than the others.

"Will it work?" she asked.

"Should," he replied.

"I guess we'll find out," Vanessa muttered.

"Is there anything more we should know?" David asked.

"Honestly, I don't know. I was studying the island with some binoculars. I didn't see any vipers but we didn't see any the first time we were over there. They were waiting for us inland. Although actually, yeah, one thing: we should expect to be attacked on the way over."

"Great," Cait growled.

"It won't be pleasant, but it's a relatively short trip. We just have to be wary. You'll have it the worst," he said, looking at Vanessa again, "because you'll have to fight and navigate the boat at the same time."

"I can handle it," she replied.

"We should plan now," Katya said, "so that we can get right to it. We want to spend as little time on the island as possible."

"Yeah," Gordon agreed.

"We should split up into two groups initially. Jennifer, Vanessa, Cait, and I will take on the hydroponic garden. Gordon, Katya, and Ruby will find the lighter and gather whatever supplies you can from the second site," David said.

"That fucking lighter," Gordon muttered, rolling his eyes.

"Condition of doing this," David replied with a shrug.

"Yeah, yeah, I know. That makes sense to me. Here." He reached behind him and his hand came back around with a large-barreled, faded orange pistol.

"What...is this?" David asked, accepting it.

"Flare gun. If you're in over your head, aim up and shoot into the sky. I'll do the same if shit's getting too heavy. You see a bright light in the sky, you'll know we need backup."

"Okay," David said. He'd heard of flare guns before, though he'd never actually seen one. He walked over to Ruby after that. "Hello, Ruby. How are you?"

"Hello, David," she replied. "I'm okay. Still some pain, but I'm up to this."

"If you're sure."

"I am."

"Okay. I wanted to thank you again for your help with the assault, and to thank you for your help here."

"You're welcome. I'm glad to be helpful," she replied. Again, he was struck by her curiously flat way of speaking. She seemed detached. Well, if she was, she was still very capable, based on what he'd seen. Maybe she was just shy. Everyone had different ways of dealing with that.

"We ready to go?" Katya asked.

"Yes," Ruby said.

They spent the next few moments getting into the boats. Vanessa did manage to fit into the bigger boat without sinking it, and he, Cait, and Jennifer got in one boat while Ruby, Katya, and Gordon got into the other one. As soon as they were all settled, they fired up the engines and set off towards the island, with Gordon taking the lead.

David and Vanessa kept pace behind him, David drifting a bit to the left, Vanessa to the right, to give each other ample room. He found himself constantly scanning the dark, choppy waters, extremely paranoid of a viper attack. Falling into the water would be a pretty bad thing right now, and this was their territory.

The first few minutes were fine, if tense.

David had ultimately passed the responsibility of steering the boat to Jennifer, who seemed happy enough to do it. He and Cait sat in front of her, their pistols out, ammo at ready if they needed to reload. David wasn't used to having to sit down while shooting. Maybe, he let himself hope, though not believe, they would make it to the island without running into any vipers. He hadn't really seen any recently, and he took that as a good sign.

The first hundred meters or so went by without a problem. The engines hummed, surprisingly quiet for what they were, and the boats glided across the surface of the frigid lake. David continually sought evidence of anything swimming in the waters around them. Cait leaned forward suddenly and he tensed.

"I think I see–"

A viper burst out of the lake's surface in a spray of icy water, shrieking wildly.

"Fuck!" Cait screamed, sticking the pistol in its

face and squeezing the trigger twice. She blew half its head off and sent it back into the dark depths.

But it was like someone had sounded the dinner bell, because suddenly the water all around the three boats was churning.

"Faster!" Gordon screamed back at them, and then they were all firing as a few dozen vipers emerged from the water, grabbing on their boats. David fought to stay upright as he stuck his gun barrel into the face of a black-eyed viper right next to him. He fired a shot, then turned and shot another one twice more. The boat rocked violently as more and more of them grabbed on. The next few moments were a confused blur of frantically shooting as many of them in the face as he could manage as quickly as possible.

He put down a trio of them on his side and sensed a presence at his back, twisted around, and barely managed to put a shot into the open, ominous, tooth-stuffed mouth of another as it reached for him, and its brains were violently ejected out the back of its misshapen skull as it slumped back into the dark waters, quickly disappearing as the boat raced onward.

With a moment to breath, he took aim and shot two of them in the back over on Vanessa's boat, as she was having her own trouble. He began to take aim for a third one when another abruptly popped up right in front of him right as he squeezed the trigger and got its head blown off.

David hastily reloaded as his pistol ran dry and fired off another half a magazine putting down the next group that showed up, trying to climb onto his boat. He could hear the others firing off a great deal of bullets as well. The island, at least, was rapidly approaching. David went through another magazine before Jennifer suddenly began slowing them down.

He looked around as the last of the vipers were killed off and they made their final approach to the island. Doing a quick headcount, he saw that everyone was still where they were supposed to be and no one seemed to be injured. He let out a long breath in relief.

They hit the island a little bit later, having to bring the boats right up to the shore itself. As soon as they grounded them a little, they hopped out, weapons at ready, and performed a quick survey of the immediate area. There were a lot of trees in the area, obscuring the view beyond the initial shore. There was only one way into the forest that was immediately obvious, which had to be the path they'd been told about.

"Come on," Gordon said, and began striding up the beach after no more vipers came after them.

David and the others followed after him.

For the first few moments, there was silence. The dead, snow-capped trees looked the same as the forests he had been spending so much of the past few weeks wandering around in. He checked to either side of him as he moved down the path with the group, paranoia creeping through him. Given the sheer amount of vipers they'd run into in the water, he found it very hard to believe that this island was abandoned by them.

Even as he looked around, he thought he saw movement farther on among the trees, but it was impossible to tell without stopping and staring, which they didn't have time for. They hurried on until they reached the split.

"Remember, flare gun," Gordon said.

David nodded, and then they split up. He and Vanessa took the lead up the right trail that would take them towards where the hydroponic garden gear was supposed to be, with Cait and Jennifer in tow. They remained silent as they moved up the path, trying to find a balance between speed and safety.

The trees were thick here and it made visibility pretty bad for anywhere but ahead and behind. He kept thinking he saw things out of the corner of his eye, but genuinely couldn't tell if it was just the trees shifting by him as he moved forward or vipers hopping among them, or if it was something else entirely.

He'd put his pistol away and was now holding onto an assault rifle. It was probably one of the best pieces of hardware they had in their arsenal now. It was a black military issue rifle with a scope, a thirty round magazine, and burst-fire or full auto selection. He'd snagged six spare magazines for it after checking it over and making sure it was functional. David had to admit, he was a little eager to see it in action.

He'd grown an affinity for guns over the course of his life. They were exceptionally useful tools against those that wanted you dead, human or inhuman or undead. Although he was often reluctant to resort to using them against those that were still alive, he had zero problems with blowing away any undead that wandered into his view.

Especially now that they were roughly ten times as lethal as ever before.

Finally, the pathway came to an end, stopping in a clearing that held a house. A fancy house, by the looks of it, though obviously no one had been here in a very long time. Dead vines clung to the siding and most of the windows were long since smashed out, the wood rotted in several places. David scanned it over carefully, looking for telltales of those horrible vipers, or anything else for that matter, but he couldn't see anything.

"Okay," he murmured, studying the two main structures he could see, "Vanessa and Jennifer, take the detached building, Cait and I will search the house. You find the gear, pack it up as fast as you can, got it?"

"Got it," Vanessa replied. "Come on, Jennifer."

The goliath led Jennifer off towards the exterior structure, which looked like it might be a garage or a particularly large equipment shed, and he and Cait hurried off towards the house. The back door wasn't just open, it was ripped off completely, tossed onto the ground, barely discernible among the snow and the slush.

David took point. The machine gun had a little battery-powered flashlight built onto its barrel, and he took advantage of that, grateful that they had managed to find a few batteries that still actually worked.

The light revealed a kitchen area overgrown with mostly withered or outright dead plants that would come back to life when spring came around again. He slipped in and panned around with his eyes and the flashlight. Nothing alive or undead, so far. He pointed off to the left, where an open door led into a hallway, and Cait whispered an affirmative, heading off in that direction. David made for the only other door in the room. Stepping up to it, he checked the way beyond and found a living room in equally shitty condition.

A smashed television, a ripped-up sofa, signs that someone had been through at some point years ago, using the place as a temporary home. He moved through it, past smashed-out bay windows that looked out onto a driveway, the forest, a rusted-out car, and a basic road that led deeper into the island, then met Cait at the hallway.

"Found a bathroom, a closet, and a guest bedroom, all clear," she said quietly.

"Okay, second story," David replied, both of them looking up the stairs near the front door at the head of the hallway. They crept up the stairs, listening to them creak and groan. David tensed from the noise, but nothing came to investigate. They got up to the top and quickly poked through another bedroom, a bathroom, and an office area. Nothing. They regrouped back at the front of the stairs. David felt like this was a pretty good place to check for supplies, as it looked relatively untouched, and was eager to dig in.

"Let's check on the others, then we can start conducting a real search," Cait said, and he nodded in agreement. They hurried back down the stairs and walked outside. The side door to the garage was open and they poked their heads inside after giving a little warning call. It was too easy to get spooked and shoot someone on accident in situations like these.

"How's it going?" David asked.

"Excellent," Jennifer replied, and swept wide her arms, indicating the hydroponic garden setup that was inside the garage. "This has everything we need. I can break down the most crucial components and pack them up, and we can rebuild a new garden with this stuff and with materials that we already have."

"How long?" Cait asked.

"Twenty minutes?" she replied.

Cait winced. "Can you cut that down at all?"

"Maybe, I don't know," Jennifer replied, losing her smile.

"Try to. Fast as you can, this place is admittedly freaking me out," Cait said.

Jennifer nodded and dropped into a crouch, where she began disassembling the garden. David began to open his mouth to say something when a gunshot sounded. It was distant, but clearly close enough that it was on the island. He felt his stomach go cold and turned around, taking a few steps away from the garage. More gunshots sounded immediately. He heard the boom of a shotgun, several of them in fact, and the higher popping of pistols. Then the rattle of a submachine gun.

"I think–" Cait began.

A brilliant orange glow shot into the sky and burst maybe a hundred feet up.

"Oh fuck me," David snapped. "I'm going–"

He froze as something shrieked nearby. Cold terror splashed his body. He saw a trio of vipers emerging from the treeline by the house. No, half a dozen. He raised his rifle and heard more behind him. They might be fucked. He cut loose with a burst that ripped a good portion of the nearest viper's skull off in a spray of gore. He shifted aim, put a second one down, shifted aim, put a third one down. Vanessa and Cait stepped out as well, opening fire immediately in opposite directions. David put down nine of them altogether and hastily reloaded.

"Stay here!" he screamed. "I'll help them and come back!"

"Hurry!" Cait replied.

He finished slapping in another magazine and shouldered the assault rifle once more, opening fire as he ran towards the path they'd taken in. More vipers were there and he put down as many as he could, opening up a path as he sprinted. He emptied the second magazine as he got back onto the path, and there didn't seem to be any past that initial group. David hastily reloaded again and had to fight the urge, the terribly powerful urge, to turn around and go back to help Cait and Vanessa and Jennifer. He heard them fighting fiercely as more and more vipers attacked them. His heart pounded painfully as he sprinted away, letting the rifle hang by its strap and pulling out his pistol instead. He had to get to the others and get them back as fast as possible.

He heard some of them following him and twisted around, aiming back the way he'd come, and opened fire on the trio he saw. One shot was good and took one of them in its eye, sending it sprawling to the ground, where it tripped up another one hard enough that he heard a sharp crack as one of its limbs broke.

The remaining one kept sprinting after him, gasping and wheezing at it came for him. He kept firing, missed several shots, and finally shot it in the chest. It went down and he faced forward again, and saw that he'd nearly run off the path and into the trees. He quickly corrected his course and then hit the crossroad area where the path split.

The gunfire had only intensified up ahead and behind.

Gritting his teeth, David kept sprinting, pushing himself as hard as he could. He could hear a lot of them up ahead and wondered just how bad this was going to get. They still had to get everyone and the hydroponic garden off the island. Fuck, could they even do *that*? He fully intended to make it happen. David kept going, following the path as it twisted around, going deeper inland, and before long he skidded to a halt as the path opened up into another clearing that held what seemed to be a simple cabin.

It was hard to tell because of the dozens of vipers mobbing it.

David holstered his pistol, snatched his rifle, and switch it to full auto. "Hey fuckers!" he screamed. Several of the vipers turned to face him. He began squeezing the trigger. David hosed them down, spraying the crowd of them with the bullets, going back and forth as he stepped to the side, trying his best to get the cabin out of his line of fire.

There were dozens of the things, over fifty at least, and more seemed to be coming in from the treeline. David emptied his rifle and mowed down probably a good fifteen of the things. He ejected the spent magazine and shoved a fresh one home, then repeated the action and put down another dozen and a half or so. As he reloaded again, he saw that their numbers were finally thinning out.

Which was good, because he couldn't keep this up. He'd already burned through about half his reserve so far. David felt his reflexes and stamina being put to good use as he switched back to burst fire and began putting down vipers one by one as fast as he could. Now that he'd helped tip the battle back in their advantage, Katya and the others in the cabin were redoubling their efforts to eliminate all the vipers.

He went through another magazine and then pulled out his pistol and kept firing as fast as he could manage, snapping between targets, and emptied it as well before finally, after what felt like way too long, the tide was stemmed.

"Come on! Katya, Ruby!" David screamed as he

hastily reloaded.

The door to the cabin burst open. "Gordon's wounded!" Katya snarled as she came out, her own machine gun hefted. Behind her, Ruby came out, supporting Gordon, who was limping badly. There was blood on his right leg.

"We have to help them!" David yelled.

He could still hear heavy gunfire.

"Fuck!" Katya snapped, and they all hurried over to him.

As soon as they were following him, he turned around and began sprinting back down the path. This was exactly why he needed more conditioning, David thought angrily as he gasped for breath. He was in decent shape, but he could be in much better shape for times like these. Fuck, he had to get back to Cait. He didn't see any more vipers on the path and that remained true until he reached the crossroads.

As he prepared to head back up the right path again, the others in tow, a clutch of vipers began coming at him from the way they hadn't gone yet.

"Goddamnit!" he snapped, and opened fire on them.

He shot one in the shoulder and sent it spinning, caught another in its throat, put a round into the bulbous head of another, right between its terrifying, huge black eyes. Katya skidded to a halt beside them and took out the rest with quick, efficient bursts.

"Make sure they don't leave!" David snapped as it occurred to him that that might happen, and it would be a huge problem, because he didn't think they could get all of them *and* the hydroponic gear back with just two boats.

"We're right behind you," Katya promised, and he took off again.

David sprinted all the way back up the path, the trees racing past him in a blur. They were *still* shooting. He made sure his machine gun was ready to go and as he reached the head of the path again, he saw another few dozen of the fuckers swarming. Screaming, David took aim and opened fire, hosing them down with another magazine and putting down another fifteen or so of the bastards.

As he went to reload one of his last magazines, he suddenly sensed another one behind him. Too late. David twisted around and then it crashed into him, sending him sprawling onto his back, the magazine and the machine gun going flying from his grasp.

Roaring in pain and rage, David ripped out his combat knife as the viper scrambled atop him, shrieking, snapping its jaws. He tried to shove it off of him as he freed his combat knife, but it was a vicious, tenacious son of a bitch. He finally pulled the blade free and brought it around, jamming it into the side of the thing's head.

The force of the blow knocked it off of him as the blade pierced its brain, killing it and, apparently, making room for the next one. David heard another scrambling towards him and jerked to the right just in time to see a second beast crawling for him. He stabbed out in automatic reaction and shoved the blade into its right eye.

It shrieked and jerked back, nerves twitching, and tore the blade from his hand. Shouting in rage again, David grabbed his pistol and barely managed to bring it up and fire a shot off before a third creature came for him. Then there was a fourth and a fifth, and he shot them both in the face and finally managed to get himself some breathing room.

Reaching out, he grabbed the knife, ripped it out

of the dead viper, and slipped it back into its sheath. He got up on one knee and took a moment to aim and put down another half-dozen vipers in the immediate area, who thankfully seemed torn between attacking him or attacking Cait and the others.

With that amount of time bought, David holstered his pistol and snatched up his rifle and the magazine he'd been trying to reload. He finished the reload as Katya, Ruby, and Gordon appeared. He opened fire, helping Cait and Vanessa put down the rest of the vipers in the immediate area. Panting, he ran over.

"Cait!" he screamed.

"I'm here, David! We're okay!" Cait called back, and she and Vanessa emerged from inside the garage.

"Where the fuck are we with this?!" Katya yelled.

"Almost done!" Jennifer called back.

David skidded to a halt before Cait and looked her up and down. She was okay. Bloody, but okay, because it obviously wasn't her blood.

"Where the fuck are they all coming from!?" Vanessa snapped as she reloaded her own weapon.

"Doesn't matter, let's hurry it the fuck up," Katya replied.

David and Cait went back into the garage, where Jennifer was hastily finishing up disassembling the hydroponic garden.

"You can grab those," she said, pointing to a pair of backpacks and a pair of duffel-bags.

They each pulled on the backpacks over their mostly empty packs that they had intended to fill up with supplies and obviously weren't going to get the chance to. Once that was done, they grabbed the duffel-bags and stood up.

"We done?" David asked.

More gunfire sounded outside.

"Almost...almost..." Jennifer muttered. David and Cait moved over to the nearest windows and looked out. Vanessa, Katya, and Ruby were opening fire while Gordon was hastily trying to patch his leg up.

"Fuck," Cait whispered. "We should–"

"Done!" Jennifer called.

"Let's go!" David snapped.

She finished shoving something into a big canvas kit-bag, which she slung over her shoulder and then pulled out her pistol.

The three of them hurried back out into the snowbound forest.

"We're good!" David snapped.

"Let's get the fuck out of here!" Katya yelled and then they were off and running.

The next few minutes were a confusion of running, gasping for breath, a blur of frozen, dead trees, and shooting at more vipers that emerged from the forest around them. They made it back to the crossroads and immediately broke left, making for the boats again. All of it passed by in a blur for David, who felt like his thoughts were skittering away from him in all the chaos. It was a seemingly impossible task to keep track of his footing, the vipers around him, the others in his party and their safety, how close the boats were...

But somehow, someway, they managed to make it to the shoreline again.

"Get in!" Vanessa snapped. She turned around and opened fire, providing them with cover fire as they hustled over to the boats. Katya did the same and took out the nearest of the vipers as Ruby helped Gordon into one of the boats. As soon as they were in, Katya shoved the boat away and then hopped up into it.

"Come on!" she yelled.

Cait and Jennifer got into the second boat, and David repeated the action, shoving their boat off the shoreline and then hopping in.

"Vanessa, go!" he yelled as Jennifer started their motor.

There were a lot of vipers still on the island. Vanessa emptied her assault rifle into the nearest ones, then ran over to her boat and began shoving it. It seemed to be stuck on something. She grunted with effort as the vipers closed in on her. David fired off the burst shots as fast as he could manage, squeezing the trigger over and over again as he switched through targets, knowing that he couldn't fuck this up, he *had* to make every shot.

His rifle ran dry.

"Vanessa, *go!*" he screamed.

"I'm *trying!*" she screamed back and suddenly the boat was jerked free. She almost fell, but caught herself and climbed up into it after shoving it farther out. David and Cait continued providing cover fire as Vanessa got her engine going, and he could hear Katya screaming at Gordon to go back and help her.

"I'm fine! Go Katya!" Vanessa yelled back at her.

And then they were heading away from the island.

David looked back as they got turned around, fully expecting to see the dozens of vipers that now lined the shore race into the water and begin coming for them. But they didn't. They just stood there at the shoreline, lining up, falling silent as they stared at them with their huge dark eyes, and somehow that was far more terrifying.

They stayed like that until they were out of sight, and only when they reached the dock again on the shore did David allow himself to begin to relax.

EPILOGUE

David looked out over the campgrounds from his bedroom window on the third floor and felt...content.

Also, fucking exhausted.

It had been a very long day.

They'd managed to make it back to the dock without a problem, and they'd gotten Gordon back to his house, where Katya took a look at him, given she had the most medical experience among any of them. Although she was still wicked pissed, because Gordon had taken off almost right away while Vanessa was still on the island. Vanessa chilled her out though, and it had turned out all right. For the most part, at least.

Katya had patched Gordon up and knocked him out with some morphine, then given Murray his lighter. Apparently they'd managed to find it before the vipers had shown up. Murray had thanked them and then they'd left after that.

David felt bad for Gordon, and those closest to him. Although no one seemed to know for sure, a bite or a scratch from the newer undead could be a death sentence. It seemed to have roughly a fifty percent mortality rate. Either you got sick, to varying degrees, and then got over it, or you died and turned.

Just another wonderful fact of living in this new world.

From there, they'd parted ways, thanking Katya and Vanessa again for the help. They had walked back to the campgrounds and had spent the rest of the day getting the hydroponic garden set up. Or, at least beginning the process of getting it set up. According to Jennifer, it was going to be a bit of a lengthy process.

Which was fine by David. He was still amazed that they'd managed to recover enough of the thing to rebuild it over here, but Jennifer said that they had succeeded in their mission. After that, they'd gathered for dinner.

That was when they had, (after privately discussing it with Evie and April and getting the okay from them), formally offered Jennifer a place in their home. He wasn't sure how she would react, but she seemed relieved, and happy.

She was thrilled to move into the basement.

For the moment, she was back in the cabin where they were setting the hydroponic garden up in. Since she technically didn't really need to sleep, she was happy to stay up all night long piecing it together.

"You coming to bed?" Cait asked, walking up behind him and settling her hands on his shoulders. He saw her beautiful, pale face reflected in the glass.

"Yeah," he murmured, and yawned. "Just can't believe we did it."

"I can. We're great as a team," Cait replied.

"Hell yes we are," Evie said from the bed.

April murmured an agreement sleepily. Tonight was a night where all four of them had decided to sleep in the same bed. After the events on the island, he felt like he needed it. He turned away from the window and took a moment to put out a few of the candles that were burning, until there was only one left, providing a gentle flickering glow to see by if they had to get up in the middle of the night and do something.

"Hey, there's been something on my mind," he said as he took his clothes off.

"What?" Evie asked.

"We don't have a name for this place. I think we should name it, since we're going to be like a real village now," David replied.

"Do you have a name in mind?" April asked.

"Yeah...we should call it Haven."

ABOUT ME

I am Misty Vixen (not my real name obviously), and I imagine that if you're reading this, you want to know a bit more about me.

In the beginning (late 2014), I was an erotica author. I wrote about sex, specifically about human men banging hot inhuman women. Monster girls, alien ladies, paranormal babes. It was a lot of fun, but as the years went on, I realized that I was actually striving to be a harem author. This didn't truly occur to me until late 2019-early 2020. Once the realization fully hit, I began doing research on what it meant to be a harem author. I'm kind of a slow learner, so it's taken me a bit to figure it all out.

That being said, I'm now a harem author!

Just about everything I write nowadays is harem fiction: one man in loving, romantic, highly sexual relationships with several women.

I'd say beyond writing harems, I tend to have themes that I always explore in my fiction, and they encompass things like trust, communication, respect, honesty, dealing with emotional problems in a mature way…basically I like writing about functional and healthy relationships. Not every relationship is perfect, but I don't really do drama unless the story actually calls for it. In total honesty, I hate drama. I hate people lying to each other and I hate needless rom-com bullshit plots that could have been solved by two characters have a goddamned two minute conversation.

Check out my website
www.mistyvixen.com

Here, you can find some free fiction, a monthly newsletter, alternate versions of my cover art where the ladies are naked, and more!

Check out my twitter
www.twitter.com/Misty_Vixen

I update fairly regularly and I respond to pretty much everyone, so feel free to say something!

Finally, if you want to talk to me directly, you can send me an e-mail at my address:
mistyvixen@outlook.com

Thank you for reading my work! I hope you enjoyed reading it as much as I enjoyed writing it!

-Misty

Made in the USA
Monee, IL
12 January 2024